The Back Building

JULIE DEWEY

A NOVEL

The Back Building

JULIE DEWEY

The Back Building

ISBN: 978-0-692-70833-0

Book design by Sabach Design sabachdesign.com

Published & Distributed by
HOLLAND PRESS
7640 Edgecomb Drive
Liverpool, New York 13088

www.juliedewey.com
info@juliedewey.com

Publisher's Cataloging-In-Publication Data
(Prepared by The Donohue Group, Inc.)

Names: Dewey, Julie.
Title: The back building / Julie Dewey.
Description: Liverpool, New York : Holland Press, [2016] | Previously
    published: CreateSpace Independent Publishing Platform, 2014.
Identifiers: ISBN 978-0-692-70833-0
Subjects: LCSH: Mentally ill teenagers--Fiction. | Teenage girls--
    Psychology--Fiction. | Asylums--Fiction. | Farms--Fiction.
Classification: LCC PS3604.E949 B33 2016 | DDC 813/.6--dc23

Printed in the United States of America

Thank you for respecting and supporting authors.

Other Books by Julie Dewey:
Forgetting Tabitha
One Thousand Porches
Cat Livin' Large Series
The Other Side of the Fence
If you like this book and you wish to join my mailing list for new releases please visit my website www.juliedewey.com
or log on to http://eepurl.com/DHWw9

DEDICATION

This book is dedicated to all those who suffer
from mental illness. It is for the friends,
family members, caregivers, researchers
and doctors who support individuals in need.

CONTENTS

PART ONE

ONE   Iona, 1915 3

TWO   Willard Hospital for the Insane 25

THREE   Reality 39

FOUR   Therapy 55

FIVE   Fatty Patty 69

SIX   Farming 73

SEVEN   Everything Changes with the Season 85

EIGHT   On the Run 99

NINE   Marriage 109

TEN   Lucy 121

ELEVEN   Lucy and Suzette 127

TWELVE   Sorrow 137

THIRTEEN   Topher 147

FOURTEEN   Cat 151

FIFTEEN   Willard Once More 159

SIXTEEN   Daniel 163

PART TWO

SEVENTEEN   Present Day 167

EIGHTEEN   Genetics 175

NINETEEN   Medical Records 185

TWENTY   Shame 189

TWENTY-ONE   Release Forms 195

TWENTY-TWO   BCT 203

TWENTY-THREE   Photographs 207

TWENTY-FOUR   Marlin 213

TWENTY-FIVE   Hanging by a Thread 219

TWENTY-SIX   Medical Records 223

TWENTY-SEVEN   Suitcases 229

TWENTY-EIGHT   Jenna 235

Book Group Questions 240

PART ONE

CHAPTER ONE

IONA, 1915

My white school blouse was speckled with tiny droplets of blood from my first victim. I had watched my father and brothers' precise alignment of traps on many occasions when I accompanied them into the woods. I tagged along under the directive that I was to "study the foliage" while they hunted. Truthfully, my mother, Esther, just wanted me out of her hair. On these forays, I was reminded that hunting was "not appropriate for women" and that "dressing the kill" was a man's job. I was told to "mind myself" while the men strategized but I found preying on animals far more interesting than cataloging leaves and their corresponding trees. So instead, I studied the men's tactics from afar, as they stalked and caught all kinds of game.

Because I was often seen in and around the chicken coop, it made sense, then, that I would set my first trap behind the ramshackle structure without arousing any suspicion. Dandelion weeds grew tall, garter snakes nested among the logs that lay in disarray, and best of all, holes were evident. I learned from watching my father pursue animals that holes were entrances to burrows. Given the fresh scat I found, it meant bunnies were currently living deep within the earth. I secured my lead wire from the knot of a log to the coop itself. I gently formed a noose and positioned it right in front of the burrow's entrance, then waited patiently.

The snare snapped abruptly and a defenseless jackrabbit squirmed and bucked its hind legs as it tried to escape from the noose tightening around its neck. I had to put him out of his misery with a quick blow to the head. I searched for a blunt object to bash in its brains and settled on a stacked log. One hit between the animal's ears and the movement stopped. Blood and brain matter splattered every which way, spraying the ground and my attire. I admired my game for a moment, and then sharpened the two knives I stole from our kitchen. I scraped the blades back and forth together numerous times, making a shrilling sound. When the sunlight gleamed from the tips, I knew they were sharp enough to gut and skin the animal. I stuck the blade into the chest cavity, piercing the warm skin, and began the gruesome process.

I wouldn't be allowed to proclaim my kill and use it for our soup, so after I skinned the animal and buried the innards, I took what little meat there was to Hetty. (I counted precisely eight hundred and ninety-two paces from my coop to her front door. When I became confused at step number two hundred and thirty-seven, I started over.) Hetty was our house-girl who lived just down the road. She was the only black person I knew and we became fast friends. My parents paid Hetty to come twice weekly and do a thorough cleaning of our home. My mother wanted our farm to be pristine and didn't have the time or inclination to get on her hands and knees and scrub the floorboards the way Hetty did. Hetty made them shine and the whole house smelled like lemons while she was working. Hetty was a large, ambitious girl who I fancied. She was seventeen years old to my fifteen, but she was allowed to eat her fill and it showed in her ample hips and bosom.

My mother wouldn't allow me to have dessert except on the first Sunday of the month, and even then it was only a simple bowl of fruit or small sliver of pound cake. At suppertime, I was given strict portions of vegetables and meat and was never allowed second helpings. Mother made me count and chew each bite at least fifteen times before swallowing it in order to get the most from each tangy morsel. The rumblings in my tummy were mere temptations, she said. Withholding food was meant to serve as a lesson that a young lady should never overindulge or give in to her cravings and desires, no matter the circumstance. Mother repeated her creed every night, "Just one spoonful of vegetables, just one helping of beef, Iona, you need to be fit and trim if you want admirers." My brothers, Greg and Michael, however, consumed second and third portions of our meal. They taunted me by greedily scarfing down their food, hardly allowing themselves time to taste the scraps on their tongues before gulping them down and mindlessly shoveling in the next bite. If they were aware of the unjust spectacle at the dinner table, they did not make any amends by curtailing their moans of delight and belches.

I wanted to slop up gravy with a thick heel of buttered bread, then smear my hand across my lips to rid the grease, and then hold my hand across my belly and belch liberally, before reaching for more. I desired the crisp, salty skin from the bird plated before us, or wads of creamy butter patted on the heaps of mashed potatoes. However, mother said to let the aroma be enough. She cupped her hands and wafted the air toward her nose to inhale the steam that permeated from the fare. She took her delight, not from the delicate tidbits of food, but rather in the men's over enjoyment of the meal that she presented.

"You'll thank me one day, Iona," she said one particular evening over supper while I stared longingly at a rack of beef smothered in mushrooms and covered in a thick, glistening gravy. I was disinclined to agree, but averted my eyes and kept quiet.

I would offer to help with the dishes and lick the plates clean of any leftover crumbs. I'd hoard the bones and suck the spongy marrow straight from them in my room at night, discarding the fragments I gnawed upon under my mattress.

The entire farce was meant to benefit me in my future. Learning how to transcend hunger and temptation, and putting the men in the household ahead of oneself was indicative of being a good and decent woman that any man would want to marry. Marriage was not something I looked forward to. The last thing I wanted was a paunchy-faced man eating his fill before me while I smiled and licked my chops. Nor did I want him sticking it to me. I knew the ways between a man and woman because I caught my brother, Greg, in the hayloft with his sweetheart, Mary Anne. Her clothes were rumpled up over her hips and her stark white legs stuck out in the air to each side making the shape of a letter "V." Greg's bare butt went up and down while he grunted and fumed, they worked hard at coming together. After witnessing the performance, I would prefer to be a spinster.

Nonetheless, there was something about our house-girl's banter and confident sway that intrigued me. I practiced moving my own scrawny hips from side to side the way she swished hers, but it felt forced and looked awkward. I was startled by the recognition that my body was starting to change. Mounds were taking shape across my chest where I was once flat. I told Hetty I would not permit this and she belly laughed out loud.

"Girl, there ain't nothing you can do to stop the mounds from growing. You might as well start getting used to them now." She grabbed and squeezed her own orbs appreciatively.

"I don't want them," I fumed, angry at my changing body.

"Most girls your age can't wait for their bust to grow. They want to know how to get them and how to make them larger.

They exercise their chests like this," Hetty put her arms out wide and demonstrated exercises meant to increase one's bust.

I didn't want a bustline that would hinder my activities. I wanted to be flat so I began wrapping linen strips tight around my chest every night to prevent my mounds from growing further. I had spindly arms and legs and never wanted to be curvaceous like some of the girls from school. Sarah Medley and Brooke Smith would fasten belts so tight around their middle, cinching their waists to appear curvy, that I didn't know how they could breathe. I hated dresses as a rule but had no choice but to wear what my mother laid out for me each morning. I always had a straight skirt, so that I looked tall and thin, a pressed blouse, and coordinating ribbons for my hair. The moment school got out, I ran home (two thousand and eleven paces from the school exit to my front door), expunged my ribbons, tore out my bobby pins, and loosened my hair. I let my curls fall in disarray around my face, alleviating the headache created by the tight hairdo. I put my school clothes on wire hangers in my closet and put on looser fitting attire that allowed me to breathe and was suitable for chores.

My mother told me I was "exasperating" when I came undone. She despised when my hair was in my eyes and blinked excessively as if she could feel the tendrils scratching her own pupils. She waved her hand in the air away from me, motioning for me to go outdoors and carry on with my daily chores. Chores instilled responsibility and furthermore, removed me from her presence. I believe she took a nip or two of brandy when I came home from school because after my chores she seemed more chipper and smelled of spirits.

I relished my responsibilities because they allowed me time alone with the animals. Brushing the horses' backsides with short repetitive strokes put me in a trance-like state. When the horses were tended, I visited the chickens. I would sit in the coop and put the hens on my lap while I stroked and plucked their feathers. (One hundred strokes each bird.) I inhaled the sweet smell of the hay and collected as many colorful eggs as I could find before heading back indoors, reluctantly.

Once inside (one hundred and seventy-seven paces from coop to kitchen), mother chided me to help with the dinner preparation. I had little to no interest in slicing vegetables, or rolling out crusts for fruit pies. The only exception was that I liked working with the raw meat. I enjoyed sawing the bones off the animals and studying their ligaments, taking note of the blue veins that, when alive, rushed the blood to the animal's pumping heart. I stripped a chicken's spindly purple vein from its thigh and ate it raw while mother turned her back. It had relatively no taste and while the texture was wormy, it wasn't the worst thing I'd ever tried. I gulped it down and felt satisfied. The raw smell of the flesh was especially tantalizing to me, which mother found disturbing. She pried me from the butchering and instead gave me the task of chopping carrots into perfectly uniform sticks.

"Iona, one serving only," my mother said expectedly when we were seated at the table for supper that evening. My stomach rumbled loud enough to be heard over the conversation that escalated between the men.

"But, Mother, I am a growing girl, surely I need as much chicken as the boys?" I whined.

"Iona, listen to your mother, one serving," my father, Don, who barely spoke to me, said without looking up from his plate. He continued, "Mother tells me you are not taking an interest in tasks that are befitting a lady. From now on, we insist that you take up your sewing after school rather than doing chores outdoors. It's time you begin acting your age and start preparations for courting." Mother rolled her eyes and reached for her brandy.

"Father, I loathe sewing. I always prick my fingers and bleed and I can never get my stitches straight." I held up my hands to show my battle wounds and scars that came from my needle and thread.

"Which is why you need to practice. Every woman needs to know how to sew. One day you will be married and you will have an army to sew for. It will become second nature for you as setting traps is for us, right boys?"

"Father, I would prefer to set traps. It is far more useful than sewing and I am good at it." As soon as the words were out of my mouth, I knew I had just blown my own cover.

"What, pray tell, do you mean, you are good at it?" His dead gaze met mine momentarily and I told him of my good fortune in catching a rabbit with my first trap.

"Well, I studied you and the boys while we were last in the woods and I came home and set a snare. I caught a rabbit, skinned it, gutted it, and gave the meat to Hetty for her family."

My father and mother exchanged worried glances. Then father set his utensils down very carefully on either side of his plate. Thick, mucous looking gravy dripped from his knife onto the linen tablecloth but he didn't notice or care.

"Hunting is forbidden for you. Do you understand?" Father stared at me levelly, fingers combing his beard to a point just below his chin.

"No, I don't. I don't understand why I am treated differently than the boys." I refused to be intimidated and my disobedience started an ugly quarrel.

"You are our one and only daughter, Iona. We expect that you will act accordingly. You will no longer accompany us under the guise you are studying the foliage. You will stay indoors and learn how to become a homemaker and proper young lady."

The boys snickered as I was being shamed, but I'd like to see them thread a needle and sit still for hours while being forced to sew.

"There will be no more of this talk, Iona. From now on when you come home from school, you will shadow your mother in all of her activities. You will sew, cook, correspond with family, press the laundry, and take up charitable work. You will no longer roam freely across the property. It appears giving you this freedom was a bad choice on our part. This is not up for discussion or debate, the matter is now closed." Spittle formed at the corner of his mouth as he spoke.

Father picked up his knife and fork and dove greedily into his large portion of meat and mashed potatoes. He kept his eyes on his plate, glaring at the bird in such a way that made me think if it weren't already dead he would have killed it then and there.

I asked to be excused. Pushing back my chair and scraping it across the wooden floors, I retreated to my bedroom (sixteen paces from the table to my doorway). The lace curtains that adorned my windows billowed in the breeze. I could hear the sounds of the outdoors beckoning me. However, I knew when my father made his mind up there was no changing it. I would just have to be more clever, that is all.

I hoped and prayed Hetty was not in trouble for taking the meat I delivered to her. My mother paid Hetty to clean, not to be my friend.

Now that I was ordered indoors, my mother saw Hetty as her ally. I also reckoned she saw Hetty as a way to get me out from under her. On the days when Hetty was working, I was told to follow her every move so that I could learn how to launder and press seams properly, and clean everything from the floors to the bathrooms. I studied Hetty's movements when she worked, and watched the sweat drip down from her brow as she rocked forward and back while she scrubbed the rust-colored mildew rings that stained our tub.

"Why do you do it, Hetty?"

"Do what?" she answered, not bothering to pause in her work.

"Clean. Sew. Swish your hips." I asked, while picking off the scab on my knee causing it to bleed.

"Well, first of all, I ain't got no choice in the matter. If I wasn't working here, I'd be working somewhere else. I got to earn my keep. I hand my money right over to my daddy and he pays our bills with it. Keeps a roof over our head. Besides, I am a woman, so why wouldn't I?"

"I don't know. I just don't like it. I have no patience for sitting still and sewing or writing letters to people I don't even know. It's downright painful." I showed Hetty my blisters from writing so many letters the afternoon before.

"Want my advice?" Hetty asked.

"Yes."

"If I was you, I'd go on acting any way that pleased my folks so you don't have to get no job. Not everyone is as nice as your family to the people they employ. Now listen, I also think if you gets real good at writing letters, maybe your mama will let you walk them to the post office in town. Now that would get you out the house for a little while anyway, wouldn't it?"

"I suppose it would, Hetty. I just feel backwards. I like being outside and snaring animals, that's fun to me. I want to learn all about tracking and hunting. I want to land a buck and learn how to gut it and smoke the meat. I want to wrap myself in its fur and be proud that I shot it. I want to chop firewood and build things. I want to be around the horses and the other barn animals. Being inside sucks the air from my lungs, I feel trapped, like I can't breathe."

"How old is you, girl?" she asked, her eyes growing dark with worry.

"Fifteen, why?"

"Girls your age should be starting to fancy boys, not out hunting and being wild, or thinking they can be independent.

Now listen to your parents. They be good people and you be causing them stress if you don't do as they say. I thought you like to read? Go stick your nose in a book and let me do my work or else you gonna get me in trouble."

I grabbed my copy of *Pollyanna* by Eleanor H. Porter and sat in the drafty hallway to read as Hetty continued with her arduous chores. I couldn't focus on the cheerful main character in the book while Hetty did all the backbreaking work. I watched as she wiped the sweat from her brow and upper lip. She finished cleaning the tub and used the towels that hung behind our door to wipe down the dirty sink before she started on the baseboards and floor. I put the book down and moved to help her with the floor. She handed me a rag and showed me how to dip, ring, and scrub, starting with the dust-laden baseboards and moldings. Next, we tackled the corners and then worked our way out so nothing got marred.

When we finished in the bathroom, I was exhausted and my arms ached. This work was not easy. Sitting and sewing was boring, but not physically taxing. I understood why my mother handed the work over to Hetty so willingly. It was worth the small amount of money she doled out weekly to have the chores done for her.

When I asked my mother about this she replied by telling me how rich people had maids who helped with the household work. The woman's primary job, then, was to oversee the daily matters of the home. The woman decided what to put on the menu for dinner, what social engagements they should attend or host and whom they should invite. Their lives were lavish and fun and I could have that if I played my cards right. My mother told me I was an unmatched beauty, and that next year, I would begin my social calendar. Until then, I needed to hone and refine my skills as a gracious young lady. She piled books on my head and commanded me to throw my shoulders back and down as I walked across the parlor ten times without dropping the novels.

"To help erect your posture," she said, leaving me to perfect the preposterous balancing act alone (twelve paces to the edge of the rug and twelve back).

I felt badly for Hetty. When she went home, it was to a clapboard house with seven siblings, three of whom she shared a room with. She didn't have a mother anymore and took on the burden of caring for the smaller children, as well as working both outside and inside the home. Often times, my mother sent laundry home with Hetty so that she could earn a little something extra. Hetty always accepted the extra work and said she was saving her money for some day down the road.

Hetty was the exception to the rule. She wanted out of our small town of Ithaca, New York. She confided in me that she had a dream to be a teacher one day. A black teacher, now that would be something.

I never thought much about my grades. I assumed they were useless if I were just to be married off when I was ripe anyway. Hetty was different. She was driven by the words her mama had instilled in her as a child. Her mama told her, "Hetty, you focus on a dream and you work hard to achieve it. You are one determined girl and you are gonna do fine in life." Her mama was teaching her to be independent and not rely on a man to make her whole.

Schoolwork came easy to me. I understood numbers and was good at adding and subtracting sums. I did most of my work in my head, but when I had to showcase it for credit, I followed the teacher's diagram on how to arrive at my answer. I enjoyed reading as long as the book wasn't about romance or ideal women.

I received glowing grades, but my teachers remarked that I had few, if any, friends in the class. They went on to suggest that perhaps my mother should arrange social engagements with my peers to help me get along better in the classroom. My mother did just that. She abhorred the notion her daughter could be socially awkward, especially when said daughter was so beautiful.

In fact, my mother told herself that it was my physical beauty that kept the other girls from being friendly toward me. She thought they were jealous. In reality, I was happier playing marbles with the boys at recess, and I was especially good at stickball. I didn't care if I skinned my knees or got my dress dirty, so the boys let me play. I was even captain once or twice and selected our players systematically, ensuring a winning team.

The girls shunned me. They laughed when my hair was falling from its ponytail, or strewn from a perfect braid after an enthusiastic game. My grass-stained knees created a stir and caused the girls to point and stare at me, then snicker as they stood huddled together in a circle, casting me out.

I didn't care one way or another. I had Hetty for a friend now and that's all that mattered. She called for me after school on Tuesdays and Fridays and together we walked toward my home, the Mueller farm.

On one such occasion, I reached out and held fast to Hetty's hand. It was plump and rough with calluses and caused a stir within me when I grasped it. She smiled deeply at me and we swung our hands in unison as we walked alongside the gravel road that led up to our fence. I hopped the fence and ran ahead of Hetty, not telling her my plan. I quickly set three traps in the woods that lined our property and would check them tomorrow. I had stashed a knife yesterday in the exact spot so if I caught anything I could skin it for Hetty. Then she could grab it for her journey home after work. With such a big family to feed, any meat was welcome.

My traps lured two squirrels and another rabbit, which I knew Hetty was particularly fond of in her stews. I would ask mother if we could spend time in the garden this afternoon, pulling up some root vegetables and be sure to give my friend enough for her supper.

First, I had to kill and gut the squirrels, then the rabbit. Hetty came upon me then and she looked none too pleased.

"Child, what in the hell are you thinking? You know you gonna be in trouble for this."

"Hetty, these are for you, I just need to clean them real quick and you can get them on your way home for supper. I thought you'd be happy."

"Iona, I could always use extra meat at the table, but you gonna get yourself, and me, in trouble and I don't want none of that. No sir."

Hetty walked away and ahead of me. I finished my job and marked the fence post nearest the catch with an "X" using the chalk I stole from the classroom.

Hetty acted peculiar all afternoon, shooing me away when I tried to help her work. I noticed the next morning however, that the meat I offered was gone. I knew it was Hetty who took it too, because the "X" was smeared and the dirt on the ground was smoothed over to mask the blood and guts.

When I saw my friend on Friday, I just smiled and ran ahead as usual (six hundred paces from the school doorway to my traps at the far end of our property). Again, I had a good catch and set about gutting the animal's entrails. I knew Hetty hated this gruesome work because she told me so when she was teaching me to cook.

"Rinse and pat your meat, like this, Iona. Iona, pay attention to what I tell you. If it's wet when you add it to the pan it is gonna splatter all over your clothes and you can't get no grease stains out, girl. Blood hard to get out too." She was teaching me to cook, but I was only vaguely paying attention.

She flinched when she said "blood," and then she told me about the time her daddy cut his hand real bad and couldn't prepare the chicken for dinner. Her brothers were out working so she had to wrangle the bird, snap its neck, and then pluck it dry. The next part was the worst, skinning the bird nearly made her pass out.

"It was like holding a baby child in my arms, when it was all naked like that. I ain't never doing that again, nuh-uh. No, sir, I'd rather be hungry."

I laughed out loud, envisioning Hetty with her head turned sideways away from the chicken, her nose turned up while she plucked the bird one feather at a time.

The next day was my first scheduled "social engagement." My mother entrapped her dear friend, Judith Taylor, to invite us to enjoy tea and scones with her daughter. Anne was a year my senior and one of the girls who shunned me at school. (I lost count at two thousand paces from our door to theirs.)

When we arrived at Judith's spacious village home Saturday afternoon for our visit, we rang the ornate doorbell. True to my mother's expectation, a maid answered the door and saw us to a room that was adorned with two settees facing one another with a coffee table in between. (Ten paces from the entrance to the davenport.) When our hosts appeared, they were both dressed lavishly in floor-length skirts and freshly pressed lace blouses with silver-embellished buttons. Judith wore a brooch at her neck that my mother fawned over and Anne played the role of gracious hostess with ease.

"Iona, do tell us how your school work is coming along. You are in the ninth grade, correct?" Mrs. Taylor inquired.

"You know I am in ninth grade…" I started to say with too much attitude.

My mother cleared her throat and nodded at me in such a way that told me I had better rethink my answer.

"Why yes, Mrs. Taylor, I am doing well in school. I can only hope to be as bright and well liked as your Anne is someday." I blinked excessively as I spoke.

"Iona, you are quite lovely yourself. I have no doubt everyone agrees." Mrs. Taylor sipped Earl Grey from her dainty teacup, her pinkie extended outward. Then the cup was placed back on its saucer and she edged it away from her as if one sip were appeasing enough.

Our conversation continued with me being sickeningly sweet and praising Anne at every turn. My goal was to make Anne be nice to me at school and get my mother off my back.

Anne did invite me to join the girls in their circle the next day at recess. She made a point to invite me right in front of our teacher, who seemed very impressed with Anne's thoughtful gesture. As I approached the circle (eighteen paces from my desk to the girls), clutching my lunch pail by my side, she quickly turned her back to me, closing the circle's gap. Anne snickered to the group and once again, I was cast out. This time I felt humiliation worm its way into my cheeks, coloring them with a blood rouge.

Every day henceforth, this game ensued. Anne pretended to be my friend when the teacher was in view, but as soon as she was otherwise engaged, I was mocked and treated poorly.

"You'll never have any friends, you little brat, and neither will your mother if she keeps begging you off on her acquaintances," Anne spat the horrific words at me one day in front of the other girls and I could feel the bile churning in my stomach as my skin warmed once again.

"Who would want to be friends with you anyway? You're nothing but a spoiled rich girl. Have fun at your sewing circles," I replied.

I would get her back and I knew just how. She could taunt me all she wanted but when she made fun of my mother I had a prickly sensation creep up my back that I couldn't let go. After school that day, I checked my trap. I had snared a squirrel that I carefully gutted. I took its limp heart out and put it gently aside. I then wrapped it in leaves and carried it home, leaving it in the toe of my boots by the front stoop. I carried my boots to school the next morning, aware of the forecast of rain and the dense puddles that could ruin my patent leather shoes.

I arrived early in the classroom and positioned my boots and umbrella in the hallway by our coat hooks, as did the other students who prepared for the inclement weather. (Twenty-seven paces from hallway to desk.) Mid-morning I asked to use the restroom (thirty-six paces from desk to bathroom) and was excused. I quickly but quietly retrieved the organ and found Anne's lunch pail. I unwrapped the slimy, un-beating heart and deposited it in between her slices of bread along with her cheese and crisp maple bacon.

I bet it wouldn't taste half bad if it were pan-seared and doused with salt and pepper. I went back to the classroom and focused on my schoolwork. When Anne's class was excused for lunch, I waited for the shrill, and when it came, I played dumb.

The prank was blamed on one of the boys, but interestingly, Anne never encouraged me again in front of our teacher. Nor did she extend further social invitations and I was more than fine with that. My mother, however, was befuddled. She had inquired about lunching with the ladies and starting mother-daughter sewing circles but no one was able to partake.

About this time, I noticed mother's belly was swollen and protruding. There was going to be a new baby within four months. They didn't know if it was a boy or girl but the doctor said mother was healthy and would have no trouble birthing this baby, although she was thirty-six.

Hetty was hired for three days a week now as mother grew larger and less able to move about freely. She waddled when she walked and tired very easily. Greg and Michael were given more duties on the farm and spent more time hunting in order to prepare our stores for the brutal winter months ahead. Ithaca was known for its damning, dreary winters.

It was during one of their hunting forays that they found my traps. They immediately relayed the information to my father, who wondered who would have the audacity to hunt on his land. Each one of his seventy-five acres was his and no one had the right to hunt on it without his direct permission.

It didn't take long for my father to realize that the simple snares were set by me, and what ensued scarred me for life. Father called me to the kitchen (eighteen paces from the parlor to the kitchen table). Holding my latest catch in his hands, he unloosened the snares and set the dead squirrels down. Mother sat by the window, her loom in her hand as she embroidered a pillowcase for the new baby. Stress showed itself in the wrinkled brow that presented across her forehead as well as her shallow breathing.

"This is madness. You deliberately disobeyed me, Iona. You are causing your mother stress due to the reports from school saying you are causing mischief and now this. We have a new baby coming soon, we can't have this type of thing agitating your mother now."

"I can explain."

"I don't want to hear your explanation. I assume Hetty is to blame, that you are giving the meat to her family, am I correct?" White spittle formed at the corners of his mouth when he spoke and I couldn't take my eyes from its foam.

"Yes, I am giving it to Hetty. But she didn't ask for it, Father. I just know it's hard for her, isn't that being charitable?" I would use any angle I could to get out of this.

"You have a good heart, Iona. But you can't put meat on everyone's table. Your only requirement is to worry about you. You are meant to become a young lady, but by all reports you are a tomboy and a social outcast. Your behavior is intolerable." Father loomed above me and tried to regain his composure.

This hit me like a brick. I felt the sting and weight of my father's words and saw the way it weighed on my mother's slumping shoulders. I had never thought of myself so harshly and frankly didn't strive to be like everyone else. I wasn't sure what I could do but the thought of running away occurred to me. I could run to Hetty's. They would take me in; I could put food on the table every night there.

"You must conduct yourself in a way that befits this family. The boys have made very good names for themselves, but you're embarrassing them and us with your ill temper. Your blatant refusal to take up tasks that are fitting for girls your age is unacceptable. If it keeps up, Iona, we will send you to my brother's farm in Elbridge and I can assure you, he won't be so tolerant. Now shape up." Finally, he wiped the creamy foam that collected at the corners of his mouth.

Later that night, I was tucked properly in bed. My hair was brushed and braided, my clothes were laid out for the morning, and I listened as my mother and father conversed in their bedroom below my loft.

"It's madness, she counts every pace everywhere she goes, and if she loses her place, she has to start over. She counts other things too, like the number of slats of wood on the floors, how many grains each slat has, the frames in the windows, the windows in the house, and so on. Yesterday, when there was a snarl in her hair and she lost track of counting her strokes she threw the brush across the room, putting a hole in the wall. She cleans the bathrooms twice a week, is fastidious about working her way from the inside out. She has no friends and refuses to act like a lady. She has no patience, Don. I am worried about the baby. You saw how she strangled the chicken last week. What if she hurt the baby? What if she is truly mad and needs help?" My mother sounded borderline hysterical. She cried in bursts that altered between strangled sounding sobs and silence.

I held my tongue as they discussed exaggerated incidents. No harm came from my counting, it's just something I did for amusement. I admit I tried stopping but found it difficult. Counting occupied my mind and I liked it. I did strangle a chicken, but that was because Hetty said it was needed for dinner. She hated the killing of animals so I offered to do it. I snapped its neck and laughed as it ran around for a count of thirty seconds before succumbing to its demise. I supposed it was true, I was an outcast, but I had no recollection of throwing a brush through the wall. That was just a lie brought forth by my mother's condition. Of course I cleaned, I cleaned with Hetty enthusiastically, to help her and learn from her as they suggested. Did they forget it was their command that I shadow Hetty whenever she was working? I needed to hone my skills, and who better to learn from than our housekeeper?

As I lay listening to my folks, I seethed and grew angry enough to spit nails. I ripped my braids apart and grabbed lumps of my hair, pulling it out in thick segments. I bit my lip in order not to scream from the pain each pluck induced; the biting produced a vast amount of blood that spilled down my chin and onto the collar of my nightgown, soaking through the fabric and leaving a stain for Hetty to deal with.

In the morning, I had fifteen noticeable bald patches on my now-lopsided head. My mother swooned when I appeared in the kitchen, but my father sat me down.

"Are you ill?" he asked, leaning over me studying the missing contents of my swollen head.

"No, Father, I am not ill, and I am not 'mad' either as you and mother suggested last night."

"Well, I don't know whether you have seen yourself this morning or not but you are missing half your hair." Father ignored the fact I overheard his conversation and carried on fussing over my hair.

My mother wept softly into her kerchief at the loss of my hair. She always said I had the most beautiful, lush, thick locks and that I was lucky. Now the hair was stuffed into my pillow with the down from our deceased chickens.

"You will not go to school today, Iona. Instead, I am taking you to see Dr. Morgan. I think we need to see what is going on here. Maybe there is a reason behind this pressing madness."

A tear escaped and I let it trail down my cheek and my chin and drip onto my clothes. I was ordered to bathe and dress (fourteen paces to the bathroom). Then we would head into town and get to the bottom of my "condition."

After being poked and prodded, questioned and humiliated, I was deemed "unwell" by a doctor who hardly knew his head from his arse. Whether or not my illness was a physical or mental matter was in question and needed further investigating. I was not allowed to attend school in either case, both to protect the good name of my family and to prevent the spread of any disease, should I be harboring one. The hair perplexed the doctor the most. The missing clumps were random and, he said, no one in their right mind would subject themselves to that type of bodily harm or pain. It was indeed painful, but I would never admit it.

My father didn't tell my mother the doctor questioned my sanity. Instead, he told her I was to stay at home and get plenty of rest. I had an unidentified illness that would benefit from proper nutrition, extra portions of meat, and lots of rest.

My mother complied with the doctors' orders and began to give me second helpings at suppertime over the course of the next few weeks. As a result of proper nutrition, I gained weight and my hair grew back in. It formed spikes in patches across my head and I liked the feel of it so much I took my mother's shears and cut the rest of it off to match.

When I entered the kitchen the following morning, my mother took one look at me and fainted. My father ran to her and cursed me. The doctor deemed me mentally ill advised that I be sent away.

CHAPTER TWO

WILLARD HOSPITAL FOR THE INSANE

I was allowed to bring one suitcase with me to the treatment facility in Willard, New York. In it, my mother carefully packed everything she thought I would need while I was away. I would be gone for one month during which time the change of scenery and care of the specialized doctors was supposed to make me "better." The Willard State Hospital on the eastern shore of Seneca Lake was known as the best, particularly for disturbed women and children.

Neatly folded one on top of the other were my nightgowns, underwear, socks, two skirts, and their corresponding blouses. Beside them, were a Bible, my toothbrush, a hairbrush, and ribbon. Peculiar, I had no hair to use the ribbon on, and my time away was supposedly temporary. There was a small sewing kit, two small needles and two spools of thread. No scissors. My indoor slippers sat on top of the clothing, and the blanket I had had since my birth was on top of my toiletries. At the last minute, my mother added stationery and a pen. She hoped I would write and promised to do the same.

A black automobile pulled up at eight in the morning on October twenty-ninth. Two stodgy gentlemen dressed in tweed suits entered our home and one took my suitcase. It was placed in the trunk of the car (twenty-six lengthy paces from hallway to trunk). The other man escorted me outside quickly, in case my parents changed their minds. My mother's hug lingered, she kissed my cheeks and her tears melted into my skin; for a brief moment I even felt loved. My father was emotionless, he spoke to the men quietly and watched from the window as I was led away by the elbow.

I did not understand what it meant to be mentally ill. I felt fine, unabridged in both mind and body. I was aware of myself and my surroundings and didn't suffer any breaks from reality. I didn't feel overly sad or happy, or even angry. My parents simply didn't understand me. I liked my new haircut and the freedom from its previous weight around my neck, and I saw no reason why I shouldn't wear it short. I did my counting in my head so no one was bothered. I wouldn't miss the constant nagging to be a perfect young lady, but I would miss Hetty. She was the only friend I had in the world and I made a vow to follow the doctors' orders so that I could get back to the farm, and back to her.

The drive to Willard took less than one hour. Situated along Seneca Lake, the hospital and its surroundings were quite pretty except for the imposing barbed wire fencing all along the north side.

"The fence was put in place to keep the thieves out." The larger of the two men said, sensing my distress. He told me thieving migrant workers had thinned out the gardens, so they put up the fence to keep them from whittling down the food stores. Also, in recent years people came in droves to witness the lunatics in the asylum, as if they expected to see patients with two heads. I felt satisfied but stunned by this honest answer, and suddenly grateful for the fence. I didn't wish to be heckled by oglers.

We drove along the lakeside and wound our way across two miles of road leading from the gate to a massive brick building.

This was Chapin House, which served as the administration building. Here, I would be given my room assignment. I would be placed in the south wing where all women were housed. I was not considered severely disturbed so I would reside on ward number three. The more disturbed patients were on wards one and two, and the back building housed the insane patients who could no longer function in society. The female administrator smiled hopefully at me when she learned my attendant would be Emily Black. Emily was known for her kindness, her understanding, and especially for her charges' good manners and cleanliness.

"Pardon me, miss, but my suitcase hasn't been retrieved. May I please have it?" I suddenly grew anxious that my possessions were out of my sight. Nerves were getting the better of me and I felt that I could be sick at any moment. I bit my nails and tasted the blood.

"It will be brought to your room as soon as we go through it. We need to catalog all of its contents, I am sure you understand," she said to me dismissively.

"Oh. Okay." I took a deep breath and stood up feeling woozy. I grabbed the edge of the desk to secure myself and then felt more stable.

"Now, then, let's show you around and get you to your room." The administrator stood up and led me out of the small office space she inhabited and through the main building toward a large hall. I tried counting the paces but found it difficult because of all the corners and hallways.

"Look around. Everywhere your eye can see is part of the Willard Asylum, excuse me, Willard Hospital. The property sits on over six-hundred acres. The land is used for everything from a working farm, piggery and its slaughterhouse, to a dairy, vegetable gardens, and a firehouse. We have a beauty salon, a chapel, a bakery, laundry, and we even have a hall solely for entertainment. Here it is now; Hadley Hall has a bowling alley and theater too. Do you like to bowl, Iona?"

"I have never bowled before, ma'am." I said, feeling overwhelmed and shy. I was missing my family and the familiarity of my own home and farm and could hardly get excited about bowling.

"Well, it also has a projection room, a basketball court, and a snack bar. We even serve hot buttered popcorn on movie night. You'll like that."

"I am sure I will," I muttered, more for her benefit than my own.

"Here we have Elliot Hall, over there is the Campus Hospital, and off in the distance you can see a few of our houses. That's where the superintendent stays as well as the steward." She pointed out the buildings that surrounded us.

"What's that building?" I asked, pointing to a shorter brick building that was rather unremarkable.

"That's nothing that need concern you. Now, here we are at your hall. The third ward is located on the third floor. You'll have no trouble remembering that."

We walked through a large set of double doors. The windows inside were large and expansive, letting in a bounty of light. Iron grates protected them from the outside with military precision. The administrator led me to an adequate room (eighty-six paces by my first count from the building entrance to the room). The room was a nine-by-eleven foot space and for now, I had it all to myself. The mattress looked brand new and I had a wardrobe and small desk. The furniture was not overly decorative but it had enough flourishes that it felt homey and comfortable as opposed to institutional. I imagined it was all made right here on the campus in the sewing room and wood shop.

Inside the wardrobe hung five sets of dresses. One dress stood out from the others because it was slightly fancier. I assumed this was my Sunday church attire. There were four full suits of underclothes, two pairs of shoes and one pair of slippers. There was also a pretty shawl in a light blue color and a hood with a hat. I was confused because I brought my own clothing with me, but these outfits seemed to be my size. I reached out to feel the cotton gowns and I supposed they would be comfortable enough. I thanked God that they weren't made of scratchy wool like a few of the ensembles left in my closet at home.

"I'll leave you to your room for now. Emily will be here shortly to meet you. Enjoy your time here." The administrator closed me into my room. I thought her parting comments were an odd thing to say to a patient. I wasn't on vacation. Although my parents insinuated that I should relish my much-needed rest and relaxation, away from whatever stresses I had.

I sat in the corner of my room, knees pulled to my chest and cried. Loneliness crept in all around me and my heart broke in two.

A half an hour later, a gentle knock came at my door. I wiped the snot from my nose and rose to answer it. A woman, who I guessed to be in her thirties, was standing before me with a welcoming smile. She held out a thin pillow and its case as well as a set of towels and sheets.

"Hi, and welcome, I am Emily. I will be your attendant while you are here. If there is anything you need, anything at all, please let me know. How about I help you make your bed up?" (Emily walked five lengthy paces from doorway to bed, it took me seven paces, but her legs were longer.)

Together we unfolded the sheet and spread it across the mattress, then pulled it taut over each of the mattress's four corners. Emily fluffed my pillow and stuffed it inside its case. Next, she walked toward my wardrobe and reached inside to grab the blanket that I hadn't noticed laying beneath my clothing. I studied Emily's movements. She was very deliberate with everything she did. I liked her right away. She was missing her right eyetooth, which caused me to stare briefly, but otherwise she was just normal looking. Her hair was held up in a bun of sorts and she wore no make-up. I noticed the smattering of freckles across her nose and thought she must spend a good amount of time outdoors to acquire them. She was probably a gardener.

"Shall we get acquainted then?" Emily asked, plunking herself down on my bed.

"I guess." I reached for the pillow and held it defensively across my lap.

"Tell me about yourself, Iona, is it?" She met my eyes and stared, but it was an accepting kind of gaze, not one of sympathy or scorn.

"Well, I am fifteen and in ninth grade. My best friend is a girl named Hetty. She doesn't go to school anymore, but still has dreams of being a teacher one day. I don't know how she is going to do that with her workload. Hetty helps my mother around our house. My mother is due to have a baby soon and because I am causing her stress," I pointed to my nearly bald head of hair, "I was sent here."

"Ahh, I see. Well, it's my job to make you comfortable here. I want you to feel welcome and so do the other girls. You are among the youngest I've ever had on my floor. Most of the women are older and I will warn you now, they aren't all as astute as you are. Many are from very poor backgrounds and have no schooling. Still, they are a very welcoming bunch. As a matter of fact, we have our art class in an hour if you would care to join. It would be a good opportunity to meet the other patients."

"I guess I would like to go," I answered, surprised by the invitation and insinuation that I was smarter than the women who were older than me.

"Good. I will give you time to settle in a bit and get acquainted with the facility. The bathroom is just two doors down if you need it. You won't be bothered otherwise. I'll come get you when it's time to go."

"Emily?" I asked, feeling vulnerable.

"Yes, Iona. What is it?" She placed her arm gently across my shoulders.

"I need my suitcase. They haven't brought it to my room yet, and it has my things. I just want my things."

"I will look into that for you, okay? For now don't worry, your things are safe." She quietly closed the door behind her and I sunk into my thin mattress. I tightened my grip on my pillow, holding it to my chest and worried.

There were seven girls, and myself, who went to the art participation class. (Counting paces was too difficult because I was busy sizing up the women.) Today we were making collages. We were instructed to cut out pictures that appealed to us from magazines and then adhere them with glue to a canvas. I thumbed through a June edition of "The Delineator" from Butterick. The magazine mostly consisted of women's fashions and rules of etiquette. Nothing interested me so I dispersed it into the common pile before my fellow charges and me.

I made it a point to keep my eyes in my new magazine, "Good Housekeeping", because one of the ladies in our group was growing irritated by something she saw. She started ripping the pages from the magazine and shredding and throwing the pieces she tore. She cried into her palms and began scratching and clawing at her skin like a wild animal, drawing blood. She seemed inconsolable, but then Emily reached for her hands and held them tightly together. Emily stopped the woman from hurting herself further and was able to calm her with her soft reassuring voice and by redirecting her focus to another magazine entirely.

I learned this woman's name was Mary and that she suffered from depression. Mary was subject to fits such as these regularly. The woman beside me was a chatty thing; she introduced herself as Ruth and claimed she was a grand duchess. Her duke was on his way to rescue her and would be here by nightfall. She described her castle in great detail from the grey stone turrets to the moats and recounted the silk gowns and jewels that waited for her upon her rescue. I listened empathetically, thinking how dire her circumstance was. It was no wonder why she was here and no wonder Emily said I was more astute. Some of these women had no sense of reality whatsoever. It was apparent that I was more together than the women I just observed, giving me hope my stay truly would only last one month.

So far, I knew Mary and Ruth. None of the art group participants were young like me. The lady across from me had one blue eye and one brown eye that I couldn't help but stare at. She said I reminded her of her daughter. I later learned that her name was Patty, and that she had delusions of grandeur. Not only had she never been married, but she certainly didn't have any children.

Everyone progressed with her collage except for me. I couldn't find one single picture that appealed to me so instead I began to draw. I drew a forest lush with trees and animals. I sketched the outdoors, it was where I belonged and I wondered why this was so wrong?

After class, we lined the hallways with our projects as I had done as a child in grade school. A few of the women behaved as children, skipping and whistling through the corridors as they admired everyone's work. I came to understand that they had regressed to this state after traumatic incidents and that it was best just to play along with them.

"Ladies, if you wish to use this time to rest in your rooms please do so. Otherwise, the lounge is open for refreshments. Everyone is welcome."

I paused at my door, but Emily walked toward me and said, "Would you like to join me for a snack? Perhaps some of the younger ladies will come to meet you."

"Yes, I am hungry." I felt the rumble in my stomach and realized I hadn't eaten since breakfast and it was well into the afternoon. (Sixty-three paces from my room to the lounge.) I had a hot cup of tea and three pastries. Emily and I sat alone in rocking chairs side by side, overlooking the lake in the distance. The view was nice. I saw a pier that stretched far out into the water and watched several people wandering down a pathway along the edge. There even appeared to be benches and picnic tables.

"We'll go there for a picnic tomorrow if you'd like," Emily said, noticing the spot in the distance where my eyes gazed.

"I'd like that." I wanted desperately to go there now, to be outside and sit still in the sun.

Just then, a disheveled patient shuffled into the lounge. Her attire was clean, but she looked as if the cat had been sucking on her hair all day. Of course, my short spikes must have appeared off kilter as well.

"Hi. I'm Rose Mary. I heard someone close to my age was here," she said, putting out her hand for me to shake.

"Hi. I am Iona. How old are you?" I asked while extending my hand in response. I watched as she piled her plate high with food from the spread put out for us. I smiled at the new friend I had made and felt hopeful that my month-long stay would not be so boring after all.

Rose Mary was prey to seizures. She had epilepsy and needed a place where she could be confined and taken care of properly.

Her family didn't have the means for a live-in nurse so this was the next best option. She ate her scones, licking her pointer finger and then dabbing it on the crumbs and licking them clean. Rose Mary brushed her hair out of her eyes and I could see the violet hollows beneath them exposing her exhaustion. Emily left us alone to go check on her other charges.

"I am sweet sixteen. So, did you meet the other cuckoos yet?"

"Ha!" I laughed out loud. I was so happy to hear her confirm my initial thoughts.

"Only a few. I met Ruth, Mary, and Patty. The others kept to themselves during art class. Ruth is too much."

"Wait until you see her tonight. She will be all made up and waiting to be rescued from this hell." She gestured half-heartedly to the lounge surroundings.

"That's so sad," I said. "How long has she been waiting?"

"For over a year now. But she never gives up hope." Rose Mary shook her head sadly.

"Wow. That's a long time to be here. I hope to be out of here in a few weeks," I admitted.

"Now it's my turn to laugh. You aren't going anywhere in a few weeks. I have been here for three years. So have most of these ladies. We are all told it'll be a month, then six months. A year at most."

"Well, I'm not, um, sick like you are. I just don't agree with my parents. I am here to get help with that and then I am going home to be with my family," I said stoically.

"I hope so, Iona, I really do." Rose Mary suddenly looked very dazed and drool dripped down her chin. Her convulsions came on slowly at first, then I watched in horror as her body twisted and contorted itself on the ground. Emily and the other attendants came running as I screamed and they held Rose Mary in such a way that kept her from hurting herself.

"Everyone, snack time is over. Please retreat to your rooms. I will gather the group when it's time for supper," Emily said, addressing all the patients in the lounge.

"Just because Rose Mary is having a fit doesn't mean the rest of us should be held prisoners in our rooms," one of the woman said glaring at Rose Mary with disdain.

I looked her up and down, not sure if I cared for her selfish attitude. Couldn't she see Rose Mary was in dire need of medical attention?

"What you looking at, kid? Huh?" the woman asked me directly.

Emily stood up from assisting Rose Mary and walked toward the other patient. Her name was Sam. She later told me she was born into the wrong body; she wanted to be a boy, but was instead a girl. She wanted to be housed with the men and felt her confinement with the women was the worst humanly possible assault against her.

A loud knock, different from Emily's, forced me awake. I answered my door and was surprised to see Rose Mary standing before me.

"Can I come in?" she asked, clutching a handkerchief with her left hand.

"Sure," I said, opening my door wider to allow her entrance.

"I am sorry if I scared you before, my seizures, they come out of nowhere sometimes. I should have warned you." She dabbed her runny nose and folded the handkerchief where it was now damp.

"It's okay. Are you alright, though?" I asked sitting up. I admit that seeing her in such an uncontrollable state was unsettling for me.

"I am fine once they're over. I get really tired from the adrenaline but at least I am back in control now. When I have a seizure I can't control anything, I am sure I must look really weird."

"Scary. That's how you looked." I did my best impression of her eyeballs rolled up into her head and tongue hanging down. Rose Mary let out a loud laugh and then I did too.

"Iona, I hope you are the one who really does get to go home in a few weeks. You seem pretty normal to me. Except for your hair. Why did you cut it?"

"I just got so mad and pulled a bunch of it out, then I wanted it all to match so I cut it. There was no harm done to anyone but myself. Still, my parents are embarrassed and think any girl who would want short hair is crazy," I admitted.

"I understand that, my parents were always embarrassed around me. I would have seizures in church or in the salon and my mother was useless. She just cried as I rolled around on the floor, but really, I know she hated her friends seeing me that way. They sent me away because there is no cure for epilepsy. I could be here forever, who knows."

"Jeepers. I feel really bad for you. It's not like you're crazy and yet you're stuck here in the hospital. Well, at least there are classes, and movies, and things to do, right?"

"Yeah, I suppose. I am learning to keep a positive attitude. Well, I'll see you later, I am getting tired again but just wanted to apologize." She stood to leave.

"Please don't apologize, and thanks for coming, that was nice," I said, grateful for anyone who dared to show me that I existed.

The day and night passed uneventfully. Emily led us to supper in the dining hall. We had a seating arrangement and I was pleased that Rose Mary was placed beside me. Our meal consisted of braised pork, applesauce, and biscuits. We even had fruit cups with sweetened cream and then tea to finish off our meal.

Emily said good night to all of her charges and told me that breakfast was at eight o'clock in the morning. She also told me that my appointment with Dr. Macy was scheduled for nine o'clock.

The creaks and settling sounds the building made didn't allow me much sleep. I felt very much alone and was scared. I wanted my blanket for comfort but hadn't received my belongings yet. I would ask the doctor if I could please write to my parents tomorrow even though correspondence is forbidden in the first week. I felt I didn't belong here and this was an emergency.

CHAPTER THREE

REALITY

In the morning, I walked from my room to the communal shower, covering my private areas with the small towel I was given, and feeling ill at ease. I counted and noted my paces as usual. The spray from the nozzle was sparse and cold, and worse, anyone could come in and see me naked. I shampooed my scalp as quickly as possible, and then soaped my underarms and feet. Rinsing thoroughly, I wrapped my body in the scratchy towel and was in and out of the shower in mere minutes. Back in the privacy of my room, I donned one of the dresses that hung in the closet. The dress fit fine, it was billowy and gray, neither of which I minded. If anything, it made me look younger than I was, but that was okay.

Breakfast was comprised of sausage links, pancakes, and maple syrup. We also had a tall glass of milk and fresh fruit. My mother would never permit me to eat so lavishly, but then, mother wasn't here. I ate my fill and felt more than satisfied. I stared at the clock, noting I had fifty minutes before my appointment with the doctor. I had fifty minutes to contrive a way to convince him I was better off at home, with my family. Granted they didn't want me, but I would change. Forty-nine minutes.

Finally, Emily came to escort me across the square created by facility buildings to Chapin House. The administration building was also the place where the doctors assessed their patients.

I sat in a sterile waiting room alone, fidgeting with my hands and biting my nails until they bled. Finally, one of the two office doors opened and a man appeared before me. He held a leather-bound journal to his chest that presumably held my paperwork. According to the sign across his doorway, this man was Doctor William Macy. He was stout, wore glasses, had a mustache that curled slightly at the ends, and smiled wholeheartedly at me. My heart dropped as he smiled, for I smelled a trap.

"Iona, what a pretty name. Please come in to my office." He stepped aside like a gentleman and let me enter before him. (Five paces from chair to chair.) His office was tidy and sparse. He had an oak desk and matching chair, a hook behind the door for his coat and hat and two extra seats pushed against the wall.

"So, tell me, how is everyone treating you so far?" His eyes lingered on my shaved head for a moment too long.

"Just fine." I said, trying to be brave.

"Forgive me. I didn't properly introduce myself. I am Doctor Macy. I have been the attendant in charge for two years now. You have been assigned to me as case number 2,343. But I prefer to call you by your name, Iona." The doctor stood to shake my hand and I did the same.

"Now that we are acquainted, why don't you tell me as much as you can about yourself? Your likes and dislikes. We'll just get to know each other a little better today, okay?" he asked.

"Well, I like to be outside."

"Good, very good." He took out his steel pen and began his copious note taking in the notebook.

"I don't like to be inside." This should have gone without saying but I felt the need to spell it out since I was feeling claustrophobic.

"Okay, understood. What is it you like to do outside?" he asked without looking up from his pad of paper.

"I like to take walks. I like the fresh air. I like to be with my family's horses, and with the chickens. I like to hunt, and my family thinks that is improper." I crossed my arms in my lap and held them close.

"Tell me about the chickens; are they your responsibility then?"

"Well, I collect their eggs. Did you know the color of the hen's ears dictates the color of her eggs?"

"I didn't know that, that is interesting," he said, seeming genuinely impressed by my knowledge of the bird.

"I like to be outside so I take a long time collecting eggs. I sit in the coop and tell the birds stories and I sing to them sometimes too."

"So, would you consider the chickens to be your pets?"

"Sort of, I guess, yes."

"It says here you pluck their feathers and that you strangled one? Tell me about that." He pushed his glasses up further on his nose and looked directly at me. His eyes penetrated right through me, making me uncomfortable.

I looked down at my white knuckles. "Well, it was Hetty's job, but Hetty doesn't like blood. I told her I would do it for her. One time she had to wrangle a chicken and pluck it, she really didn't like the work at all. I don't mind the task so I did it for her."

"You don't mind even though they are your friends, or pets, rather?"

This felt like a trick question. "Well, sir, Hetty is my friend, too. Either way, the chicken in question was going to be served for dinner that night, so I just offered to save Hetty the trouble."

"I understand. Tell me about Hetty then. What is she like?"

"Hetty is funny. She tells me some good jokes that make me laugh."

"Where did you meet? How did you meet?"

"She works for us two days a week. She does all the hard chores like scrubbing floors and the baseboards, as well as the tub and toilet. She does the laundry too. Her hands are always cracking and bleeding from her calluses."

"If I understand correctly, your parents employ her to work. How did the two of you become friends when she is so busy working?"

Another trick. "Well, my mother wanted me to shadow Hetty because she is such a good worker. She always gets the rings out of the tub and the floors shine when she is done with them. The laundry smells good and fresh and is always properly pressed."

"I wish I had someone like Hetty!" He laughed.

"Yes, she is really nice to me too."

"How so?"

"Well, she has patience with me. She never yells at me when I scorch a shirt or dump a pail of water by accident. She just tells me to learn from it and do better next time."

"She sounds very wise. How old is Hetty?"

"Hetty is a few years older than me." I liked talking about Hetty, but it made me sad too because I missed her something fierce. A tear welled up in the corner of my eyes and threatened to spill down my cheek.

"You look sad. What's wrong, Iona?" he asked with true empathy.

"I just miss Hetty. I want to go home," I admitted.

"I know you do. What would you do differently if you went home?" There it was, the question I had been waiting for.

"Well, I would listen to my parents and become a proper young lady. I would cook and sew and do whatever else they wanted. I would mind them better," I said.

"I understand you have a new baby coming into the folds of the family soon?"

"Yes, and I want to be there to meet him."

"Him?"

"Or her, but I think it's a boy. My mother mostly has boys."

"I see."

The doctor closed his pad and put the top on his pen. He told me he'd really like it if I stayed a while longer. He thought I would start to like the facility once I got used to it. He also told me I could volunteer anywhere I wanted in Hadley Hall, the entertainment building. I would think about it I told him. Then I was released to Emily who sat outside the office waiting to bring me back to the ward. We took a detour through Hadley Hall and Emily showed me the bowling lanes. I was interested to try the sport so I lifted one of the balls, but it was so heavy that Emily laughed when I tried to roll it down the lane.

"Tomorrow we have bowling, there will be lighter balls then. These are set out for the men!"

She showed me the cinema room, the theater, the basketball court currently being used by ten men playing an intense game, and finally the snack bar. We filled cups with popcorn and nuts and walked back to the third ward.

"So, did he tell you about our new patient?"

"No, he didn't, why do you suppose he would?"

"Well, she is your age. Her name is Kate and they are trying her out on the third ward since you're here. The doctor hopes that being with someone her own age will help her."

"In what way?" I asked wondering what this Kate needed help with.

"I am not really at liberty to say, let's just hope it all works out. She'll be arriving tomorrow."

"Hmm, okay. That will be good I guess, I already have one friend, but two would be good."

"Oh yeah, who did you connect with?" Emily asked.

"I like Rose Mary. She's really nice."

"Rose Mary, huh." She didn't say anything else but soon enough we were full from snacks and I was told we'd be taking a trip to the chapel at eleven, so to be ready.

I put on the nicest dress and shoes from the closet and waited until it was time to go to church. My suitcase with all my clothes still hadn't come and I had forgotten to mention that to the doctor. It irked me that someone was going through my things and I wanted them back. I wanted my stationery so I could write my parents, double gosh darn it. I forgot to ask about that too.

I couldn't sleep, so I just fidgeted while I waited for our chapel trip. Finally, it was time to go. We walked down the steps and through the second ward, a route I had not taken before, (one hundred and seven paces). Patients were more vocal on this level and I even saw two of the staff holding down one young woman with blood smeared across her forehead.

"Never mind about that, they are doing their job, understand?" Emily told me.

"Uh huh," I said, but I didn't like how the patient was being restrained at all. I needed to get out of here before that happened to me.

In addition to our group, a group from the men's ward attended the service. The men were all much older. I guessed by their gray hair they were all in their sixties. Some of them drooled and others closed their eyes and slept during the sermon. It was a little unsettling but soon enough it was over.

After church, my group went outdoors for recreational therapy. We were allowed to walk along the property and would resume with a picnic by the lake. Just being outside helped me to settle my nerves.

We had drumsticks and cornbread along with carrot sticks and celery. I took my lunch to the lonely wooden bench and sat eating while I looked across the tranquil lake. It was very still today, and the sun glistened off the water. The leaves were changing color and the air was crisp, I felt optimistic in this moment. I knew I could get home if I could get my hands on some paper. I knew I could survive a few more days and felt hopeful indeed. I ran my hands through my short, bristly hair and wondered what possessed me to cut it? My mother said my hair was among my greatest physical attributes. Maybe that was why I did it, so that my mother would see me, not my hair. I would discuss this with the doctor at my next appointment. Funny, he never once mentioned my hair, or lack thereof, today.

When our picnic was over, we walked the long way back to our residence. I admit I did feel refreshed. Perhaps the methodology of recreational therapy worked after all.

The new girl arrived and was assigned to be my roommate. She had a bed in the opposite corner from mine but we shared the wardrobe. She was just lounging on her elbow, biting her nails when I twisted the doorknob and opened the door.

"Ha, ha, ha!" she blurted when I walked in. "What happened to you? You look like a boy!"

"Nothing happened to me. I cut it," I said, perturbed both by the fact this new patient was in my room and by the fact she was so bold.

"You look ridiculous," she said.

"I don't care," I retorted.

"Is that why you're in here? You are not to be trusted with scissors?" She laughed.

"You could say that, what are you here for? Being rude?"

"Good one. No, although I am prone to violence. I am here for my lack of self-control."

"Never heard that one before. But then again I just got here."

"I was at Utica's Insane Asylum before being transferred here. Thank God, I need some new prospects."

"I am afraid to ask," I said, gulping down the bile that was rising in my throat.

"Boys, stupid. I need some poor unsuspecting boys, or men, doesn't matter, to fall madly in love with me. Then I'll have my way with them." She grabbed my pillow and began mauling it.

"I don't understand."

"You will. You're still young. I'm Kate, by the way, but everyone calls me Cat." She laughed and then opened the door and walked out like she owned the place. I followed her only because I was looking for Emily. I wanted to ask about my suitcase and stationery.

"You following me, kid?"

"No, I am looking for Emily." She was the second person who called me "kid" and that bothered me. Emily rounded the corner and approached both of us.

"Well, it sure is nice to see that the two of you have met. We will head to the theater for a movie in an hour if either of you care to join. Otherwise, you may have relaxation time in your room."

"I do," I said and I swore Cat mimicked me under her breath.

"Um, Emily. I have to ask you something," I said, trying to keep my voice from cracking with emotion.

"Sure, Iona, what is it?" Emily studied me with a look of concern.

"Well my suitcase hasn't been brought to my room yet and there are a few things I really need. Can you please find out where it is?"

"Iona, sit for a minute. I sense this is troubling to you. The doctors don't want new patients to have their belongings for a period of time. They don't want you focused on home, and feel that this is the best way to adapt."

"I don't understand. I just want my hairbrush and my nightgown. The one issued is itchy and uncomfortable," I complained.

"I understand, I do. Please believe me when I say there is a method to your care. This is just a small part of it. What else do you need? I will try to provide it for you."

"I want my stationery. But I bet I am not allowed to write home yet either." I knew that in fact I wasn't allowed to receive or send out any mail for at least one week.

"That is correct. Let's get you refocused. How about you pick out today's movie reel? Then you and I can go ahead of the group and get the snacks ready."

"Okay, Emily. I don't understand how that will help, but okay." I felt Emily was being slightly condescending but agreed to go along with her plan.

The first week passed by slowly. My suitcase never appeared but I had bigger problems, namely, Cat. Cat tried sneaking into my bed every night. She pretended to be frightened, but then she started caressing my back and hair. I was shocked and humiliated when she touched my skin. I just wanted to be left alone. I told her this every night, but last night, after her advances, I reached out and punched her square in the jaw, which unfortunately landed me in the doctor's office for a conference. I explained to the doctor that Cat made unsolicited advances on me at night. I told him that I asked her repeatedly to stop, but that she insisted I would like what she could do to me. The doctor applauded that I stood up for myself even if he didn't condone any violent behavior. He said we needed to discuss my impulsiveness at a future meeting. Cat was moved out of my room and farther down the hall so we wouldn't have any further instances.

While I was at the doctor's, he took advantage of our time and asked if I felt anything was helping me to feel more peaceful. I told him I liked the lake. I also mentioned I had made friends with Rose Mary and he praised my efforts and encouraged me to continue to meet new people. I didn't broach the subject of my belongings because I didn't want to agitate or make my crime against Cat any worse. I would have to be patient and wait a few more days.

On my way back to the ward, I saw a woman bashing her head repeatedly against the brick building. I ran to her and tried pulling her back, noting her dead eyes. Blood dripped from her forehead and nose. The woman struggled against me and became irate. She screamed and spat at me, cursing and gesturing wildly with her arms. I let her go and several aides rushed to assist her as she staggered backwards. She really was crazy. God knows I wasn't that dire. The image of the woman with her bloody face and vacant eyes stayed with me all through the night and I recounted the situation to Rose Mary that evening after supper.

"I am sorry you had to see that. That was probably Sally. Her husband and two children died in a fire and she has never been able to get over it. She punishes herself for it every day."

"Why would she do that?"

"Because she set the fire. She's a pyromaniac."

"Jesus," I said because there were no other words. I suddenly wondered about my safety at this place. I had to get a message to my parents that I wasn't safe here and so I begged another patient to borrow some stationery and began to write my letters home.

Dear Mother and Father,

I am terribly sorry for all the stress and hardship I caused you. I promise to obey you in all matters and to do my best to

become a proper lady. I will make an effort to make friends and will not complain about any social engagements. I wish to come home. Please let me come home.
Your loving daughter,
Iona Elizabeth

I sent my first letter the second week of my stay at Willard Hospital for the Insane. I didn't get a response so I drafted a second.

Dearest Mother and Father,
Please forgive me for my past digressions against you. I have learned better how to handle myself now and feel that I am ready to come home. I would like the opportunity to prove to you that I am better.
I also admit that Willard is frightening to me. I don't always feel safe here among the patients, many of whom are prone to violence or throwing fits. It is not a suitable environment for a girl my age.
I miss you all.
Iona

I sealed the envelope and put the stamp I borrowed from Ruth on the upper right-hand corner. I was heading down the hall with my letter when Cat stopped dead in her tracks in front of me.

"Why do you bother with that? You know they don't mail the letters don't you?" I was startled, what could she mean they didn't mail the letters? It was my second week so mail was permitted.

"You're lying," I said, and tried to move past her.

"Am I?" she asked, eyebrows raised and jaw set.

"Yes. There is no harm in sending a letter. You are a liar, that's what you do, you lie. Now move," I said, hands tightening their grip on my envelope.

"Have you heard from home yet? I didn't think so. That's because they haven't received your letters, either that or they want to forget all about you once and for all. The freak of a daughter they so unfortunately had that put a blight on the family name." I reached out and grabbed Cat by the neck. I shoved her head into the yellow painted cinder blocks that lined our hallway and didn't relent.

Emily ran down the hall at top speed, yelling for me to stop. Rose Mary came out of her room and just stood watching. Ruth opened her door to see what was happening, but closed it at once. No one else really cared. I was reprimanded once again for reacting to Cat's taunts in such a volatile manner and was given my first warning. Warnings were followed by write-ups and then patients were moved to the next level of care. In my case, if I continued on this path I would be moved to the second ward with individuals who were more troubled.

I took the opportunity to ask the doctor if my letters were mailed and he assured me that yes, they were. I didn't trust him entirely or the facility and it's method of care. More than ever, I needed to get out.

Emily urged me to try harder. She seemed to care about my welfare more than anyone and didn't make me feel edgy or nervous like the doctor.

"I tell you what, let's have a picnic by the lake again tomorrow. Would you like that?"

"Thanks, Emily. I would like that." I would look forward to it and until then I would plot a way to get home.

I wrote a third and fourth letter home over the course of the week, asking, or rather, begging my parents to respond to me. I asked them how Hetty was and told them I missed her presence. I asked about the baby and signed off with love as always. I didn't hear from my mother but by my fourth week at the hospital, a letter arrived from my father.

> *Dear Iona,*
>
> *We have received your letters and have had correspondence with Dr. Macy. He tells us your violent spells have become worse and that you are in no shape to come home.*
>
> *I would ask you not to torment your mother with your letters. She is only now starting to realize how much you needed to be treated. She is recovering from the guilt she has felt and I ask that you allow her this peace.*
>
> *Yours,*
> *Father*

My heart broke all at once. A fountain of tears cascaded from my eyes and did not cease for hours. I cradled my knees and rocked back and forth on my bed, alone. I had never felt so betrayed or unloved. What had I done that was so ghastly that my parents would send me away and ask that I not correspond with them? I was sorry I acted irrationally and cut my hair, sorry for setting traps too, but nothing deserved this treatment. Surely not my counting spells.

I decided I would write instead to Hetty, my only friend and ally. I didn't know her exact address but the postmaster would get my letter to her. Also, I would write to my mother once more. If she wrote to tell me she didn't want my correspondence then so be it.

Emily checked on me regularly during the week trying to motivate me to take part in activities with the other patients.

When I refused to leave my room, she scheduled an appointment for me to be seen at once by Dr. Macy.

"Iona, I understand you are overcome with melancholy. Please tell me what I can do."

"Yes, I am sad, Doctor Macy. I had a letter from my father." I reached into my pocket and retrieved the crumpled note so the doctor could read it for himself.

"It seems pretty clear to me that your parents just want you to get well. Iona, take part in the process and then maybe you can go home."

"Maybe?" I asked, nerves getting the better of me once more.

"Well, we have some things to discuss yet, some topics I had hoped not to delve into until you developed trust in me and faith in our institution. Now that trust is shattered because you have seen that your parents and I correspond. Now you feel betrayed. It is true, I did tell them you had a few occurrences that were not entirely your fault, but nonetheless, they did occur. Is this a false statement?"

"No, it's not." I still didn't trust him.

"Let me tell you a story about our very first patient at Willard. Her name was Mary Rote. She arrived on October thirteenth of 1869 by steamship. Several men had to escort her down the gangplank because she was both deformed and demented, and unable to walk without assistance. Her hands were chained together. She was considered a 'lunatic' and had spent the previous ten years in the Columbia County poorhouse in New York.

"Let me back up for a moment. Dr. Willard, whom our hospital is named after, was appointed at the time to research the conditions of facilities that cared for the criminally insane. He drafted a questionnaire that he sent to each and every county judge in New York State. The judges then handpicked respectable medical professionals to carry out inspections of poorhouses, almshouses, insane asylums, and jails. They answered the questionnaire and returned them with their findings directly to Dr. Willard. His research found that in the fifty-five counties there were one thousand, three hundred and fifty-five chronic cases of patients who were deemed insane. Furthermore, the conditions in which these individuals were kept were described as deplorable and unfathomable. These patients were neglected, abused, and mistreated, both emotionally and physically.

"As a result of this study, the Willard Bill, which regulates insane asylums, was put into effect. This is how this hospital came to be and one of the underlying laws was that the criminally insane be treated with better care. We call this moral treatment. I am morally obligated to treat you, Iona, with respect and the utmost care I can deliver.

"Now, back to Mary Rote for a moment. When she arrived here, she was deformed and who could blame her for becoming despondent and demented after the treatment she received? For ten years, she was held, against her will, naked, deprived of food, and chained to a wall at all times. She stood no chance of healing, yet, once she arrived here she was taken in and bathed. She was treated with kindness and grace. She was given her dignity back. She was fed, she was shown to a warm bed, and do you know what? She improved markedly.

"Why am I telling you about this? Well, Mary Rote was extended an olive branch, and I am extending one to you now. I know you feel uneasy, but if you allow us to care for you using the tools that work, then we can discuss getting you home."

"I am nothing like that woman."

"We don't know why she was insane, back then if one was poor they could be called insane and be subject to an almshouse. No, you have a family who loves you and wants to see you improve. Your condition is unusual for an adolescent, but I have seen it once before."

"My condition, what is my condition, Dr. Macy?"

"I'd rather not get into that today. But I suggest that you take the olive branch you have been extended. That you agree to meet with me for some intensive therapy and then we can more thoroughly discuss your state."

"Do I have a choice?"

"If you have another suggestion, I am open to it."

"I don't."

"Well then, let's meet the day after tomorrow. I will give Emily your new schedule of appointments. I also want you to partake in our occupational therapy. This is meant to keep you occupied. We offer textiles, sewing, pottery, leather work, basket making, chair caning, and so on. You might enjoy these activities more than you think."

"Doctor, respectfully, all those activities seem rather dull and tortuous to me."

"Iona. Just open yourself to finding something you like. It will help you adjust."

Emily retrieved me and I mulled over all we had discussed. Mary Rote's story was pathetic and unjust. I wondered what she did to deserve her foul and humiliating treatment. I was exhausted and somewhat defeated and just wanted to go to bed. My eyes were swollen from all the crying I had done and Emily agreed to fetch me ice to help with the swelling. She tucked me into my bed for the night and I slept like a baby.

CHAPTER FOUR

THERAPY

I sat rather uncomfortably on the wooden chair in front of Dr. Macy who stared at me before beginning therapy. I didn't know where to look so I just stared back without blinking. I had an uncanny ability to stare for long periods of time without blinking. This was just one of the games Hetty and I played for fun.

"Let's start with why you count. Do you know why you do it?"

"No, I just like to."

"What do you count, besides paces?"

"I suppose I count just about everything. I count the wrinkles on my dress and your forehead, the panes in the windows, the hands on the clock, and the spaces between the numerals."

"Even if you know the answer, do you still do it?" He asked, laughing and feeling his forehead for a moment.

"Yes."

"Does it bother you that it occupies so much of your time and energy?"

"No. I never thought about it that way."

"Counting can be symptomatic of obsessive compulsive disorder. Some patients count, others have to do things in succession. Some wash their hands repeatedly or open a door a given number of times before leaving a space. Do you do any of those things?"

"Just the counting, but doctor it doesn't harm anyone so why is it wrong?"

"It's not that it's wrong, Iona, it's just a small part, a window if you will, into your mind."

"Okay."

"I'd like to discuss Hetty. What makes her special?" Dr. Macy asked as he shifted his right leg onto his left knee in a more casual position. I found his shifting movements to be off-putting.

"I didn't say she was special."

"Well, what is it that drew you to her and made you want her as a friend?"

Why on earth did he care so much about Hetty?

"She paid attention to me. She was nice to me."

"I understand. How did the other girls at school treat you?"

"With disdain."

"Can you elaborate?"

"They closed me out of their circles, laughed and scoffed at me, and I didn't like it. They were anything but ladylike and charming toward me."

"Why do you think they behaved like this to you?"

"Because I am not like them, I am a Tomboy. Because I like to play stickball and marbles. Because I am smarter than they are."

"You are very smart, I will give you that. Your vocabulary is quite impressive."

"I like to read, that helps."

"Ahh, excellent. We shall try to provide you with whatever reading material you'd like. Now then, tell me when exactly do you get to spend time with friends?"

This was a repeat question, an attempt to trick me up.

"I have no friends. I only see Hetty on the days she works."

"Yes, I am sorry, I should have realized that. I wondered if Hetty goes to school? If so, does she have any other friends?"

"I don't know if she has other friends," I answered truthfully. I tried to remember if Hetty ever mentioned anyone but nothing came to mind.

"Let's move on. Have you made any acquaintances here, or met anyone you deem worthy of your friendship?"

"That's an interesting way of putting it," I said.

"Well, you're an interesting girl."

"I like Rose Mary. I feel bad she is so sick, but she is very friendly and helpful to me."

"In what way?"

"She is nice, and seems to like me. She helps me get through the day because she makes me laugh."

"Laughter is important, it's said to be the best medicine."

Dr. Macy asked a few more seemingly irrelevant questions and our session ran out. We would meet again in two days' time. It plagued me why he was so curious about my friendships, what was it about them that he found intriguing enough to focus on? I thought we would discuss my parents and family more but so far, we hadn't at all.

As a part of my occupational therapy I spent the next few days participating in numerous different activities. I was mildly interested in pottery. I used the clay to mold figurines of animals and time passed quickly while I perfected my shapes. I was allowed all the time I wanted in the art studio and did enjoy it. A few other patients came to the class; one woman was so melancholy she cried the whole time as she worked the clay with her fingers. Another patient was volatile, she spewed insults to everyone and no one in particular, her language was vile and shocking. She tore at the clay relentlessly and threw large clumps at the wall to see if they would stick. I sat far away from her and was glad when her time was up and she was ushered by her attendee back to her room.

Other than pottery, I enjoyed my time walking outdoors and sitting alone by the lake. Sometimes Rose Mary joined me, but usually I was alone. If it weren't so chilly now I would attempt to swim or paddle one of the canoes across the lake.

My next appointment with Dr. Macy arrived and I fully anticipated it would be more of the same "let's get to know each other" banter. Instead, he approached me with a seriousness that surprised me.

"Iona. It's time to get to the heart of why you are here. Do you feel ready to really listen to my assessment?" he asked.

"Yes, I do, I want to know how to get better so I can go home. Doctor, please tell me what's wrong with me." The moment of truth had arrived, leaving me feeling exposed.

"Well, it appears you are delusional. In addition to this, you are rather excitable and highly emotional. You are also obsessive compulsive as we discussed earlier. The word 'delusions' can encompass many things, but in your case it has to do with figments of your imagination. I have spoken to your parents at length. They have sat in this very office with me discussing your case," he admitted.

"What? My parents were here? How come I didn't get to visit with them?" I felt irate and confused.

"It's strictly prohibited during your first month, Iona. I know it is hard, but they did inquire about your overall health and are willing to do anything to get you the help you need."

I ran my fingers through the fuzz on top of my head and rested them in fists beneath my chin. I didn't know how to feel. I wanted to spit nails I was so angry, but I also had a sudden urge to sob. I could feel my chest tighten and wanted to leave the office at once.

"Small children often have imaginary friends, this is considered fairly normal. Usually these friendships serve as ways for children to gain confidence while they grow. Or, more often, these friends are used to test boundaries. For instance, if little Toby had an imaginary friend named Ralph, he could blame an awful lot of things on Ralph. He could say, 'Ralph spilled the milk, not me.' Or 'Ralph made me do that.'

"Uh huh, what does this have to do with me? I never had imaginary friends as a kid."

"Your parents would agree with that. As a child, you were perfectly normal, you were social, adaptable, capable, and agreeable. Now that you are a young woman things have changed."

"How so?"

"Well, as in the case with Toby and Ralph, eventually Toby would outgrow his need for Ralph and the imaginary friend would cease to exist. In your case, you didn't have a need for this type of friend as a child. Now, however, you are filling some need by believing in things that aren't really there. Let's take Hetty for example. She is near and dear to your heart, your greatest friend, correct?"

"Yes, yes she is."

"Let me be frank. Hetty does not exist in this world. Hetty is very real to you, I understand that, but she is a mere figment of your imagination and nothing more. You have devised her to be exactly what you need her to be."

"That's not true. Hetty is real, of course she is real. Why else would my parents hire her? They brought her into our house, not me." This was preposterous. I could not believe what I was hearing.

"I know that is what you believe to be the truth. However, Hetty is no more real than Rose Mary is."

"No, that's not right. It's not true. They are lying, you are too." Anger welled in the form of tears and I was becoming hysterical. Why on earth would this man, who I don't really even know, be telling me all these lies? I needed air, my chest was tightening, and my fists were balled up so tight that my palms were bleeding from my digging fingernails.

"Take a minute to let it digest." He continued to stare at me in a way that made me uncomfortable.

"I don't need a minute. You, you don't know me. I am not crazy, I don't have imaginary friends. My parents just don't love me, they have wanted to get rid of me all along. They sent me here to this place so they could be alone with the new baby. Unless I suppose, you're going to tell me that I made that up too?" I realized this sounded a bit paranoid, but stood my ground.

"No, that part is real. Your mother is expecting a baby in a few months. Your parents tried to let your friendship with Hetty go, but when you strangled the chicken, they were alarmed. They fear for your safety, Iona. Can you appreciate that?"

"No. I can't and I won't. I want to speak to my parents, now." I was firm.

"I am afraid that's not possible. But if you would like to write your father, he has agreed to correspond with you. Your mother is somewhat fragile at the moment with the stress of your, er, situation, so it's best to leave her out of the equation for the time being."

"Dr. Macy, with all due respect, you are mistaken about this. You have only met with me on six occasions. Do you really feel you have enough knowledge to make such a bold, harmful, assessment?" I was beyond perturbed at this junction and realized that by speaking up for myself in this manner I could be doing more harm than good.

"I am being honest with you, Iona. Your intellectual capacity is probably through the roof, which accounts for some of your social disgraces. You speak like an adult, and read at the level of one as well. I believe it's precisely the reason for the delusions and also the reason we can heal you and get you home where you belong."

"I don't want to be pacified, Dr. Macy, with you telling me I'll be going home. Rose Mary said you say that to all the patients, yet most of them never leave."

"It's true, our population tends to stay for the better part of their lives, but we don't force anyone to stay, we often encourage it though, depending on the case. In your situation, because of your young age, we do have the right to hold you here against your will. I hope it doesn't come to that though."

My mind was spinning and I tried to understand the method and thought process that would possibly make this man hate me so much. I am simply misunderstood. Hetty is as real as he is, and the fact he would make me question and doubt the one friend I had was ludicrous. I would write Hetty once more and when she replied, I would prove to him that she was as real as the ground we walked on. I was able to calm myself down now that I had a plan. I would easily prove him wrong and then he would see that my parents lied. He would then be able to help me figure out why they despised me and wanted me out of their lives.

"Iona, Iona, I am talking to you…" he said, interrupting my train of thought.

"I'm sorry, what? I was just thinking."

"Yes, you were very far away there for a moment. Might I ask what you were thinking about?"

"I will write to Hetty today, when she writes back you will see that you have been tricked. As for Rose Mary, she is one of your patients. She resides on my hallway. If you don't believe me, ask Emily."

"I have. I am sorry, Iona, but she doesn't exist. You talk to her as if she does, I have seen this with my own two eyes upon observing you from a distance. You converse as if she were right beside you. You laugh with her and go into deep conversations with her, you choose her for your companion on theater nights and walks to the lake. However, she is not real anywhere but in your mind."

"This is absurd. I would like to go to my room." I pushed out my chair, not believing a word of this nonsense, and stood up to leave. I could not handle any more of this and I didn't want to become demonstrative. It was no wonder why the people here stayed. They were lied to and made to feel crazy by the very people they were supposed to trust.

"It's a lot to take in. Please let me know if you need to see me again before tomorrow's appointment. Until then, try to stop counting and just see what happens?"

The doctor suddenly looked older. There was a look of pain in his eyes as if he disliked tormenting me. Yet it didn't stop him from filling me with his lies. I didn't thank him, or meet Emily's gaze when she arrived to escort me back to the third ward. I stopped talking and just walked with my head down, eyes cast to the ground below my feet. I counted the paces back to my room. I lay curled up on my bed and thought of these supposed delusions. I have talked to Hetty. I have held fast to her hand. I have supplied food for her family, and helped her clean. She is real and so is Rose Mary. I rather wished Cat wasn't but, unfortunately, I have felt her too and she is not only real, but also a heartless, troubled girl.

With each passing appointment I had with Dr. William Macy, I grew more upset and unruly. His words, not mine. I did in fact try to stop counting but grew agitated and it showed. He was concerned I was becoming a disciplinary problem and offered help in the form of a talking cure that I refused. He also offered an opiate or sedative but I told him no. It was very clear which patients were on these medications because they spent most of their time in a daze. I didn't want to be comatose and unkempt like they were. One young man's state really bothered me, I saw him numerous times when walking across the property. This man was filthy and while he always looked to be yelling, no sound came from his mouth. His eyes held fear like he was trapped and unable to find any control. Like Mary Rote who was tied up and left naked all day, every day, for ten years. I refused to give up control or give in.

"The medicine will help you sleep, Iona, and it will give you some comfort so that you can acknowledge your delusions and deal with them."

"No. It will take away my humanity, my very soul in every way. I refuse to have any shots administered. I refuse." I crossed arms across my chest and stuck out my chin. I would hatch an escape plan before I allowed anyone near me with a needle.

"As an alternative I would be willing to try hydrotherapy. It's very relaxing and only involves submerging ninety-seven percent of your body in water that is body temperature. I run a tight ship here, Iona, I rarely give patients an option. I need to keep all of my patients safe, and if I think your temper puts any of them at risk I will act. Now, having said that, I advise you strongly to have Emily schedule your first bath for today."

"Emily, what are the baths like?" I asked on the way back to the ward. I tried not to count but the need to was so compelling we had to go back to the doctor's office so I could start fresh.

"The patients enjoy them and find them very relaxing. Water is known to be a healer so when the body is submerged for long periods of time, followed by cocooning, it has a calming effect." She talked while I counted.

"I am supposed to have you take me there," I stopped and replied, remembering what pace I was on, then continued.

When we arrived at the hydrotherapy station later that afternoon, (four hundred and nineteen paces) I was surprised to find I was not alone, but in a room with six tubs. Naked women of all ages stood around me waiting for fresh water to fill their bath to the correct temperature. Modesty was not evident as women with sagging breasts, sunken bellies, and flappy arms stood without embarrassment among the others. For me, waiting for our tubs to fill, while stark naked, would be the worst part of the treatment. Thermometers were attached to each tub and monitored throughout the session so that the water was kept at body temperature. The patients were submerged and covered with sheets that were then draped over them before being submerged as well. Then the lights were turned off and everyone relaxed.

I looked at the fellow patients around me, they all had pleasant expressions on their faces and closed eyes. I wondered if they peed in the tubs. I shut my eyelids and found my muscles did relax a bit and some of the pressure came off my chest. Perhaps I did feel slightly more like myself. Rose Mary entered the room and was appointed the tub next to mine. She gave me a simple smile and sank into her tub like she had done this before.

I felt my heart break for a moment upon seeing Rose Mary; she was as real to me as this tub, but what if she was a delusion? If that were true, how would I ever determine what was real in the future? Confusion wrapped itself around me, clouding my very existence.

I closed my eyes and eventually was led from the tub to a wrapping station. A nurse enveloped me in dry warm towels after two hours of soaking. One towel entombed my hair and the other my slim body. I sat quietly in an adjoining room for another hour. Finally, the treatment was over and I went back to my room. I was bored to tears, but at least I was done with treatment for the day.

By the end of the week, Dr. Macy had backed off his plan to give me sedatives. I had yet to agree I had a problem that required them, but acknowledged the hydrotherapy as being helpful. I had not heard back from Hetty or my father as of yet, but that meant very little. Hetty was most likely working overtime now that my mother was so close to her due date.

I would hatch a plan to get myself out of this place. No one here understood me or wanted to help me in a way that I thought was effective. They would rather appease me by keeping me comfortable and manageable. I needed to start hoarding food so that I had enough to get me by while I traveled. I would not go home. I never liked Ithaca much anyway, I could settle in Waterloo, Syracuse, or even Rochester. I was smart, the doctor agreed, and felt certain I could get a job as a switchboard operator, or as an artist, or maybe I could even just hunt and sell my catches to local butchers and restaurants. The possibilities were limitless.

That night at dinner, I stuffed two extra rolls up my sleeves. In the morning, I stole two hard-boiled eggs. At each meal, I left the table with something else for my food stores. I kept the food in my wardrobe, tucked inside my hat. The weather was cold now that it was November, and that brought about the realization that if I were going to run, it had better be soon so that I didn't get caught up in the snow. I could steal a canoe and paddle across the lake. I would have to tell a lie of omission when I applied for work. No one was to know that I spent time at Willard, for I would never be hired then.

I was all set to sneak out of my room. Rose Mary found me a bobby pin that I could use to pick my lock. They began locking my door sometime last week when I became less manageable. Once the lights were out, I inserted the pin into the doorknob. I got it opened without too much effort and made my way down the darkened hallway. I had my hat stuffed full to the brim with food and my pillowcase held my clothing.

The third ward did not have guards at night so I managed to creep down it successfully. I worried more about the second and first wards because they did have guards patrolling the halls. Patients' moans echoed through the second ward, guards rolled their eyes and ignored the ruckus. I walked fifteen paces before ducking into the bathroom to catch my breath. This was nerve wracking and I missed a count because I was so preoccupied. I felt compelled to go back to my room and begin again but forced myself to stay put. I peered around the doorway and when I found the coast to be clear, I made my way farther down the ward and landed in the stairwell. I rested against the cool cinder blocks for a moment, and then made a run for it through the stench-filled first ward. Two guards were on duty but lucky for me they were both occupied by patients.

I had done it. I managed to get all the way outside. I didn't know the building had night guards outside the exits and one of them saw me immediately. He grabbed me and catapulted me against the wall. My belongings were confiscated and I was taken to the attending physician. I was surprised the attending was a woman. She had a degree in gynecology she told me when I asked. She was tired and in no mood to poke through my past, she simply marched me back to my ward and alerted the entire staff that I had tried to run. Now my chances were nil. In the morning, there would be consequences, so I might as well sleep a little.

In the morning two armed guards came to my room to collect me. They escorted me to the office of Dr. Macy who shook his head when he saw me.

"You shouldn't have done that, Iona. Now I have no other option, and nor do you. You are being suppressed," he said.

Dr. Macy led me to a room with a centralized tranquilizing chair. The chair had a wooden allotment where my head was positioned. The allotment ensured that my head and neck remain still during the course of the treatment. Similarly, my arms were buckled into restraints that adjoined the chair. Bile rose in my throat as I felt the sting of a sharp needle jab its way into my arm muscle. Then, I felt drowsy and carefree all at once. I must have been carried back to my room for when I woke I was tucked into my bed, shoes traded in for slippers and pajamas on.

Emily peeked into my room half past noon and brought with her a tray of food. There was an apple and some buttered toast spread with strawberry preserves.

"Do you think you can eat?" Emily asked and I sensed her empathy.

"What happened to me?" I asked. I remembered almost nothing.

"You tried to run, and made it outside too, but then the night guards caught you. You were subdued this morning at one a.m. You are scheduled for another shot after lunch so I suggest you eat or you will have a stomachache."

"Emily," I cried, "help me." My surroundings grew hazy with fog.

CHAPTER FIVE

FATTY PATTY

When I woke once more it was sometime during the middle of the night. The ward was quiet and stillness surrounded me. My head spun and ached and I felt nauseous. Suddenly, I had a feeling I wasn't in my normal room. In fact, I wasn't. I crept out of bed toward the door and opened it slightly. I was on the second ward. I should have known by the foul stench of body odor that permeated the walls. Patients were more disturbed down here and less likely to care about their personal hygiene.

At six o'clock in the morning, a woman knocked on my door before barging in. She walked to my bed and grabbed my blanket right off me. "This is mine now. Hear me, Iona, when I say I run a disciplined hall. I do not tolerate any shenanigans." She spit when she talked at me.

I gulped and glanced at the tag she wore on her pocket, her name was Patricia. In my mind, she was "Fatty Patty." She was large and had body odor so strong it made one dizzy. I plugged my nose when she waded in closer to me to speak again. She yanked my hand from my nose and breathed her stinky coffee breath right into my face. I missed Emily. Was Emily even real?

"You lunatics have no ability to feel, so we don't keep the ward heated at night. You won't be needing this." She already had my blanket, but now she confiscated my sheets too, leaving me to freeze through the afternoon and upcoming night on a bare mattress. I would have to beg for my covers back, or steal them from someone else. This place was turning me into a convict but it was the only way to get along. I had to use my head and get back to the third ward with Emily, Ruth, Rose Mary, and the other women.

Worst of all, my nemesis, Cat, had also been transferred to this floor. The second night, she made her way into my room and asked if I needed help getting warm. She laughed and then lay down behind me. I hadn't been tranquilized in twenty-four hours so I was fairly clear headed. If I just gave in to her demands then I wouldn't have to throttle her, which would only land me in more trouble. Cat started to rub my head and nuzzle my neck. I was stiff all over and terrified of what she wanted. I knew this wasn't right and began to run scenarios through my head.

"I see you haven't found yourself a man yet," I said, although I shouldn't have.

"No need, you'll do just fine. You know the real reason I'm in here? My folks said I was too promiscuous. I would just as soon kiss a girl as a man and believe me, I have kissed both many, many times. I can't say one is better than the other." She continued to stroke my skin and moved her hands upwards toward my breasts where she began fondling the mounds that were growing larger now.

"Please stop. I don't want to do this. I will scream for Patty."

"Ha! Just who do you think sent me in here to rid you of your sin?"

"She wouldn't!"

"Patty is crazier than the lot of us put together. She thinks we're the devil's spawn."

"I said, get off of me, and get out of my room. Now."

"Or what?"

I didn't reply, I just balled my hand into a fist and slammed it into Cat's nose. The blood poured out of her nostrils in torrents and I was sure I had broken it because it swelled instantly. I opened my door and kicked Cat out.

"You'll be sorry you did that." Cat said, spitting blood on my wooden floor. I sat on my bed waiting for Patty. She came in full of steam, yanked me up by one arm and led me down a hallway I didn't know existed. She deposited me in a dank room with no furniture and locked the door. I was left there to rot for the remainder of the night. I lay on the cold floor in a ball, trying to make sense of what was happening to me.

When Patty retrieved me twelve hours later, she warned me, "If the doctor hears about this, it'll be worse next time. See, I told you I keep order on my hall. Yes I do, I don't accept any violence, and poor Cat has a broken nose now."

"She deserved it." Patty turned around and clocked me one in the gut, then the nose. Bright red blood gushed down my chin but it was the sting of the assault that shocked me into submission. I didn't think my nose was broken, but I couldn't be sure. Patty put me in a straightjacket, which made any movement impossible. She dragged me to the nurse's station, and presented me to the gal on duty. "This one walked straight into a wall." No one questioned the incident; the nurse simply packed my nostrils with cotton and sent me back to my room.

"I heard you walked into a wall," Dr. Macy said at our appointment later that afternoon.

"Yes. It was a hard a wall." I wasn't going to admit what happened, I don't know if he genuinely cared, he had three hundred of his own patients after all. He looked tired today and I knew I was the least of his problems now.

There were over two thousand patients at Willard Hospital. In addition, there were nearly five hundred employees, which is why the outbreak of bovine tuberculosis was a tremendous threat to the population. People were falling ill all over the facility.

"I've given your case a lot of thought. Normally, when underage individuals come to us we try our best to keep them amused and occupied. We typically don't allow them to work like so many of our older patients. I wonder, though, if it might benefit you." He rubbed his tie as he spoke.

"How so?" I was intrigued.

"Well, we are a self-sustaining property. The patients run the farm, the piggery, the slaughterhouse, the canning factory, the dairy, the garden, the tin shop, the broom shop and so on. Every mattress in the facility is made right here, same with the bedding, the brooms, the baskets and crates. If any of these things interest you in the least, perhaps they would be rewarding. The other option is that we do have a school you could attend on campus. Actually, you could probably teach there, because I assess you are superior to many of our teachers with your English skills.

"I want to work on the farm. Put me with animals so that I can be outside, please."

"Hmmm. I wouldn't want you harming any poultry, Iona, this is serious. We depend on our livestock for our daily food and nutrition."

"I know. Give me a chance please." I prayed for the job just to get out from under Patty's firm hand.

"Okay, I have an idea that might work. I will call the foreman and you will start tomorrow after breakfast at the stables. No more hydrotherapy during the week, we will schedule that for the weekend. And, Iona?"

"Yes?"

"Steer clear of the walls from now on, all right?" We both knew I didn't walk in to a wall, but what happened on the second ward was not entirely in his hands to control.

CHAPTER SIX

FARMING

The following morning when I woke, I noted the Edison phonograph was in our lounge. It appeared that the lucky, comatose patients of the second ward were in for a treat today. I was sorry I would miss the music but was looking forward to being outside in the fresh air and away from these cuckoos and the sadistic attendee. It was chilly, so I was given long-john's to wear under my dress. I had a hat and would receive gloves that befit whatever job I was given.

The overseer was John Hamm. I stifled a laugh at his name because it was just too ironic to be coincidental. John Hamm oversaw the farm, particularly the piggery.

I was assigned the backbreaking job of mucking out the stalls belonging to Doctor Macy's team of horses. I was experienced with horses and relished the opportunity to breathe in the sweet hay and be among creatures that didn't judge me as insane.

At noon, my job was nearly complete. I was using the hoe to place fresh straw for the beasts when Mr. Hamm came toward me with a brown paper sack.

"Here's your lunch. When you're done you can brush the horses and report back to me.

I unpacked my sandwich, it was ham. I laughed again and bit into it gratefully. There was no one here to cause me any trouble; everyone was too busy. I wondered if Mr. Hamm was a patient as well, and if so, what his ailment was. I often heard that patients were admitted because they were too "excitable" or had weak nerves, or they had schizophrenia. Some were delusional, like me, and others just couldn't get along in society. No matter I supposed, as long as he was kind to me we would get along fine.

I brushed the horses and braided their tails. I saved the apple from my lunch and fed the pair of horses each a half. They nuzzled into me as their way of saying thanks. I had a frightful thought and felt uneasy when I allowed myself to consider that this moment may not be real. Could this all be in my head? I stopped for a moment and looked around my surroundings. I could smell the hay, could smell the piggery down the road. That was something real wasn't it? I let the horses lick my palms, there was saliva on my hands when I pulled away, or was there? I wiped my hands on my coat and it appeared damp.

"Something wrong with your hands?" an unfamiliar voice asked.

I panicked; afraid I was hearing things now. Startled by the intrusion, I looked up to see a young man, maybe a few years older than me, coming my way. How could I be sure if he was real? Panic crept in causing a tingling sensation in my forearms and calves. I turned away briskly. I put the hoe away and left the barn to find Mr. Hamm. The voice followed me.

"You there. Wait a minute."

I stopped in my tracks and waited.

"My name is James, I work in the barns too, and I just wanted to meet you." He stuck his hand out for me to shake. I felt its rough interior, but I had felt Hetty's once too.

"Nice to meet you, James. I am Iona." James had a friendly face with large gray eyes that immediately caused the hairs on the back of my neck to stand up. What did Hetty and Rose Mary have in common? Why their friendly nature toward me.

"So you got to work with the princess today, huh?"

"Yes, Savannah is a beauty. I enjoyed her." I wanted to find Mr. Hamm but was drawn to James and wondered if it mattered if he was really here or not. Just then, a foreman called out for James to return to work and he left as quickly as he came. I watched him talk to several men and then go about his business. Had I ever seen Hetty or Rose Mary interact with other people?

It made me wonder. Just then, Mr. Hamm approached. "You have done a fine job, Iona. Come back tomorrow and if you continue to work hard, we will put you in charge of the stables."

"Thank you. Is there anything else I can do today?" I hated to go back to the hospital.

"Not really. I am guessing you don't want to go back yet, huh? I understand, how about if you spend another hour getting to know the horses. They need to be able to trust you for when you ride them." He smiled at me and left.

When I ride them? I was flabbergasted. Mr. Hamm said they needed regular exercised and that the superintendent only took them out on Sundays to church. Finally, things were shaping up for me here. I could get through the rough, cold, unpredictable nights if it meant spending my days here. This filled me with relief.

That night, my teeth chattered as I shivered from the cold that made sleep evasive. How could I steal a blanket? Maybe there was one in the barn. Finding a blanket became the least of my problems. Patty started checking on me hourly so the devil didn't work on me while she was in charge. She did not want me to sleep; she knew an hourly wake-up call and no blanket would lead to sleep deprivation and then my relenting. I refused to give in to this ghastly woman and her torture. Half way through the night, she fitted me into a straightjacket. "So you don't get any ideas," she said and left.

Now I was cold, tired, and uncomfortable. This was enough to make a sane person mad. I woke with a headache, but was grateful for the hour or so of sleep I received. An aide came in to undo my jacket. I stretched my arms and tried to loosen the knots beading up in my back and shoulders. I had deep, dark circles under my eyes and wondered how my day at the stables would go. I ate a heaping plate of runny eggs and bacon and reported to work.

Mr. Hamm took one look at me and shook his head. I was certain I looked worse than I felt. My short hair was now sticking up in all directions; dark puffy bags rimmed my eyes, and I shivered from the ungodly cold. Mr. Hamm gave me a warm cup of coffee and left me to muck the stalls. By eleven, I had completed the task, and could now barely keep my eyes open.

"Why don't you lie down in the hay and get some shut eye?" It was James.

"I couldn't. I have to do my job, I can't be caught slacking off or God help me."

"I'll give you a warning if anyone is coming."

"Thank you but…" I still wasn't convinced he was real.

"Look, I was a patient here too, once. I see the signs… someone is out to get you. Whatever you do, you cannot let whoever is doing this win. If you get to the first ward or the back building, you are as good as committed for life."

"Why?" I asked.

"They save all the special experiments for the lunatics on the first ward. Those admitted to the back building are rarely seen again. A few years ago they were extracting thyroids. Then last year they started heavily drugging patients to induce fevers, now they are experimenting with anti-psychotic drugs. The word is that they experiment on the patients who reside in the back building. Ever been by there?"

"No, I don't even know where it is," I admitted.

"You'll know it when you see it. The people there are like walking cadavers, some of them nothing but skin and bones. You seem normal, so I'll let you in on a little secret. No one here has your best interest at heart. No one. They just want you to be easy to manage, so if you are difficult in any way your punishment will be excessive. Now get some rest, because obviously, you are being sleep deprived."

I lay my head down in the hay in a corner of the horses' stable. I fell into a fitful slumber within minutes. Two hours later James woke me and handed me a sack of lunch. He had brushed the horses and tidied up the stalls so that when I was eating and Mr. Hamm came in, he praised my work once more. He gave me the job of keeping the stables and horses clean at all times. My hours were from eight a.m. to two p.m. I asked Mr. Hamm if he had any more jobs for me, but as of now, this was all he had.

At two o'clock, I was escorted from the stables, down the hill, across the grounds and back to the recreation center where my attendee and ward mates were scheduled to be. (Nine hundred paces from Chapin Hall to the stables.)

Several women from my ward appeared catatonic. One couldn't speak English, which didn't prevent her from trying to communicate with me. Her lips moved at a fast pace and the vowels rolled off her tongue beautifully but I was unable to understand their meanings. Pamela, the nudist in residence, kept disrobing and running up and down the hallways naked as a jaybird. She flapped her arms to mimic flight and sang nonsensical words at the top of her lungs. When the guards finally captured her they put her in a strait jacket and ushered her away. She left a stream of urine in her wake.

I had to get out of this place. I had begun to question my own sanity and felt very confused at times about reality. The horses would be my ticket out. I just needed a little time to develop a better plan of escape.

That evening during supper, Patty sauntered past me and reached for my dinner tray. She flipped it over so that all my food landed on the ground. She stepped on my meatloaf and I watched it ooze out from under her shoe. My mashed potatoes splattered across the table and down to the floor, and my string beans were in disarray.

"I wasn't hungry anyway." I stood to take my leave, pressing my hand against my growling stomach as I made my way from the dining hall to my room. I would not let this woman rile me.

"Where do you think you're going without an escort?" Patty chimed.

"To my room, care to walk me?" I asked with sickeningly sweet innocence.

"Jay, take this patient to her room." Patty motioned to an imposing black man, who got up from his seat and grabbed my elbow, ushering me to the second ward.

"She got it in for you bad. Here, eat this." Jay handed me a buttered roll.

"Thanks, Jay. She won't break me." I took the roll and crammed it into my mouth before anyone saw.

"She might. I have seen it happen many times, most of those women are now on the first and you don't want to go there. I'll see if I can intervene, but I can't make any promises."

At least now, I had an ally. Of course, he could be a delusion, I could have walked myself to my room, but then again Patty wouldn't allow that so I decided Jay had to be real.

The night torment continued, nurses came and went from my room every hour, making sleep impossible. The temperature in our hallway couldn't have been forty degrees. I was near frozen and half-starving. I missed Hetty. I missed her wide smile and boisterous laugh. I missed my family and never heard from them after father's one letter. They had dismissed me; I was fifteen and on my own in an asylum for the insane. The admission hit me full force. If I could get Dr. Macy to think I have come around and agree I had contrived Hetty and the others, then maybe, just maybe, I could leave. If not, I would escape. So now, I had two courses of action and I would plan and follow them both.

In the morning, I attempted to eat, but the nurse on duty said, "Because you ate all of Milly's food from her plate last night you aren't allowed any food this morning."

I protested and tried to explain what in fact happened, but she said she was just going by the nurses' notes that everyone had signed off on.

I got to the farm, starving, parched, exhausted and in no position to do physical labor. Mr. Hamm took one look at me and called me to his side.

"Sit."

"I can work, please let me work."

"Not until you've eaten. Why haven't you slept? You have bags under your eyes the size of Texas."

"I really don't want to talk about it. You wouldn't believe me anyway, and if you did there is nothing you could do to change the situation."

"Maybe not, but I could try. Now, what's happening?" he asked, scrutinizing me. Mr. Hamm wasn't a doctor, he was a farmer and a stand-up citizen. He was rough around the edges, he wore dirty overalls and was missing a few teeth. His hair was thinning and he had quite a belly on him. He always chewed on hay and I decided to trust him.

"The night nurse doesn't like me, she keeps taking food away from me so she doesn't 'feed the devil.' She has my blanket and my sheets too, and she doesn't let me sleep more than an hour at a time. She says I have evil in me deep and it's her job to get it out." Just being able to tell someone felt good and I began to shake as I launched into all that was happening to me.

Mr. Hamm put his hand across my shoulder. "There, there, it'll be all right," he said.

"How?" I looked up at him with fearful eyes.

"We will add a few more meals to our list for the kitchen to prepare, you can have breakfast and lunch here, and we'll give you what we can to take back for your supper. I have a horse blanket you could put under your clothing, but if the nurses are checking you every hour, they will surely notice it and take it away. I'm afraid that would get you in worse trouble. I suppose you'll just have to sleep here during your shift. No other way around it. I've seen 'em treat patients in the worst ways possible and it makes no sense to me whatsoever."

"I can't tell the doctor because that would make things worse. I can't be placed on the first ward, Mr. Hamm. I'll become a case for experiments, be poked, given drugs and worse all day long."

"I know. My wife, she was a patient here for a short time. She was treated well at first. The doctor seemed to understand her and validated that the loss of our son was indeed traumatic and the cause for melancholy. I was allowed regular visits from day one. That was part of our agreement upon her admission. I would take a job on the farm so that I could see her daily. She was all I had. My wife was placed on the third ward for women with a nurse named Josephine. Josie for short. She was kind and gentle, but then Josie caught diphtheria and could no longer work. A new nurse's aide took over and that's when I noticed a change for the worse in my wife. She became more withdrawn and cagey, she lost the sparkle in her eyes. They extracted her thyroid in hopes she would improve but she only got worse. She stopped speaking and became catatonic. She just sat and rocked a baby that wasn't there, all day. I think being here made her crazier than she was when I admitted her. They asked for my permission to perform a lobotomy, but I said no. A few days later she was dead. I think they went ahead with the surgery but I can't prove it."

"What was her name?" I asked.

"Miriam," he responded, while holding tight to his hat.

"And your son, what was his name?"

"Jacob. He was a sweet little lad of two when he caught influenza. That was years ago. But I will tell you that I saw things. Things I should never have seen, I saw men in cages and others chained to walls. I had hoped the treatment improved but maybe it hasn't. You seem very normal to me, what is the reason you are here, were you homeless?"

"My parents had me admitted. They claim I am a delusional, disobedient sinner, and Mr. Hamm, I might be. I have had a few imaginary friends that were very real to me. I don't always know what's real. This conversation, it feels pretty real, and this hot cup of tea, I know it's real because it's burning my hands. Sometimes though, I am not sure, and I don't think being here is helping me. But my parents don't want me back until I have redeemed myself."

"I see. Well, those horses are real, I can assure you if you get behind a leg and it lands a kick on you, you'll feel it and have the marks to prove it. I will help you, Iona, if I can. Now curl up and get some rest."

"But this is my job, I have to work or I'll be on the ward all day."

"How will they know what you're doing up here? No one comes here, except the doctor on Sunday. We will be sure to have his horses ready and we'll give you the credit. Won't we, James?" I did not know how long James was listening, but he looked ashamed because he was caught eavesdropping.

"Yes, sir, I will make sure of it," he replied sheepishly.

James brought me a meal of sausage and toast. Then he found me a blanket and covered me while I slept in a pile of fresh hay. I had trouble at first because I was so used to my sleep being disturbed but eventually I was out cold. At one o'clock, James woke me up to eat. I had gotten nearly four and a half hours of sleep.

"Tomorrow you will get more sleep. We're keeping you here until three from now on."

"Thanks, James." I ate my lunch and felt gratitude for these simple, kind gestures. Patty was getting into my head and I was starting to believe I was a sinner, why else would I be here. The kindness brought stinging tears to my eyes.

"I have witnessed what goes on here for ten years. They don't treat the patients right. They just don't. The lucky ones have jobs, and of course, some of the ones with jobs were never crazy to begin with, just poor."

"It's a hospital for the insane though, isn't it?"

"It is, but sometimes they take the elderly or the poor and the sick off the street and give them a bed so they don't disturb the city."

"Mind if I ask why you have been here so long?" I knew it was rude to probe but couldn't help wonder about how he got to this miserable place.

"It was a long time ago." He looked into the distance, cleared his throat and gave me a shortened version of his story. "My, uh, father, Henry, was an alcoholic. He came home drunk every night and slept all day. We were poor, so putting food on the table was hard for my mother, Joanna. My father drank away his paycheck, giving her only spare change. One night he came home and all we had was one potato to eat, he had been abusive to my mother many times in the past but this time he was out of his mind."

"James, you don't have to finish the story if you don't want, I can fill in the blanks."

"No, it's okay. I trust you, I don't know why except that the horses are so calm around you and they aren't like that with everyone. Besides, I heard you talking to John. I'm sorry for eavesdropping. I suppose it's only fair if you know my story now. So anyway, he threw my mom against the wall and she fell, hitting her head against the table on her way down. She died instantly. My dad had two of his cronies sign me over to the state claiming I hit her upside the head with an iron. He turned me in, his own son, just so he could keep on drinking. He never visited me once. I have been here since I was nine. I had so much energy when I got here and the doctor at the time took a special liking to me, he thought it would be healthy for me to be working the farm, playing with the animals and far away from the real patients."

"So, are you still a patient then?"

"No, John took me in years ago. The doctor signed me over to his care because we learned my father died a few years back. I like the farm work and John has been like a father to me anyway, so it made sense to stay. We live in Ovid, a small town a few miles down the lake. I even took his last name, Hamm, as a way to show my appreciation for all that he has done for me."

"You're lucky. Well, not for what happened to you, I am really sorry about that. It's just not fair you lost your mom. I just mean you're lucky you aren't living here anymore. Patty should be the one locked up, I've seen her douse her patients with tea hot enough to scald their skin, or deprive them of food and toilette privileges. Then she curses them for peeing themselves and writes them up as well. She is mean and nasty and I can't take much more." I had peed my own bed and now my mattress had a tangy scent that filled my room.

"She's trying to break you, Iona. Don't let her. We will help. The new superintendent, Dr. Macy, runs a tighter program than most, but with thousands of patients, even he doesn't know what's going on half the time."

"What's the worst thing you've seen?" I asked as I chewed my toast and waited for his answer.

"Well, if what we think happened to John's wife did in fact take place, that would be pretty brutal. I've seen the scoop they would use to remove the brain with my own two eyes. It was in a surgical room in the back building. I used to spy on the patients when I was a kid and I found this neglected-looking building on the north lawn behind the hospital. I squeezed my way in and the first thing I noticed was the smell of human waste. Patients were lying in the hallways, some were diapered, while others were completely naked and chained to benches and walls. There was no sign of humanity left in their eyes at all. These souls were lost. I don't know what kind of experiments they were performing on them, but whatever they did, it didn't work. There were rumors too, rumors of male patients being castrated to relieve them of their psychosis. I didn't believe it at first but then I saw a dead body when I discovered the morgue one day. I saw the body of a male patient lying on the cold table and he didn't have his, uh… Now that doesn't mean he was castrated here at Willard, but one never can be sure."

"Jeepers. That's awful. I can't let anything like that happen to me, I can't let Patty get to me." The stories made me frantic and fearful for my life.

"You won't, now go ahead and rest while I clean up around here."

CHAPTER SEVEN

EVERYTHING CHANGES
WITH THE SEASON

My birthday came and went without acknowledgment. I didn't receive a greeting from my folks or Hetty. There were no cakes or songs to mark the occasion. Only I knew the day was meant to be special. I was a sixteen-year-old young lady now, six months into my treatment, with little ammunition regarding my argument for release. Nothing changed at Willard. I felt I was more a prisoner than a patient and Patty was more suspicious than ever that I hadn't been broken. She said the devil in me was stronger than she thought.

She continued her campaign of night-time terror, she even went so far as to chain me to my bed regularly so I was less likely to try another escape. I was still hatching a plan for that but needed a little more time. Also, I was growing fonder of James. Leaving the hospital for good meant never seeing James again. Staying meant being starved and tormented but seeing him nearly daily. I wouldn't call us sweethearts, but over the past several months it was fair to say we both became fond of one another.

It was James who took me out on Savannah for the first time. My light weight on her back forced her to be unruly, rendering it necessary for James to mount behind me and take the reins. Then she obliged us very well. She sauntered across the gardens and down the path to the lake, where we often let her graze as we picnicked for lunch. I was constantly in a state of exhaustion, but James and John, as I took to calling Mr. Hamm, let me sleep from my arrival until noon. Then we ate a hearty lunch, took the horses out, and upon their return I slept more. My naps were at intervals but they had kept me from breaking under Patty's rule.

Dr. Macy asked me if everything was going well at the farm, he wondered if I found the work too taxing. Patty had divulged to him that it might be more than I could handle. She told him in her notes that I slept all the time on the ward, never interacted with any other patients, barely had an appetite and seemed to be faring worse.

I assured the doctor that, in fact, the work was so healing I couldn't imagine my life without the animals. I talked to him of his glorious horses, and how good natured they were when I took them out for a ride. I told him what and how much they ate, and I knew he could tell by their shiny coats every Sunday that they had been well cared for. He praised me for my work but suggested he'd like to stop by one day to see me ride, perhaps even ride with me. I had to be on the lookout now for his appearance at the stables and that made sleep even more elusive. Just when I would fall into a slumber I would jar myself awake, fearful Dr. Macy would appear and catch me snoozing. I was so fearful now of the first ward and the experimental laboratories that I had a heightened sense of guilt and wrongdoing when I slept.

Hydrotherapy remained a constant in my life. I became used to being naked in front of the other women even though my body was changing and becoming more shapely. I had been advised to steer clear of Rose Mary. The doctor wanted me to acknowledge but ignore my apparitions. If Rose Mary did appear during bath time I nodded in her direction but shut her out with closed eyes and a mind that was open to the fact she was not real as I had originally thought.

I began to question the reality that Hetty existed and was more comfortable that whether she did or didn't, I would be okay. I had seen so many curious cases here that my delusions hardly seem remarkable and my counting was not even noteworthy. The doctor and I discussed, at regular intervals, what importance the delusions held for me and why. We never derived an answer but the questions made me think deeply about my familial relations. I was quite alone in my home in Ithaca. My brothers were as thick as thieves and so were my parents. I had no one to run and play with, so when my classmates turned on me, I felt the sting of rejection so acutely that Hetty appeared.

I actually didn't see this as insane, but rather brilliant. If my mind could subconsciously pretend to the level of pain that being rejected caused and answer with an apparition that was needed to boost my confidence, then what was the harm? I said as much to Dr. Macy and he didn't disagree, just said we needed more time to think this through so it didn't happen again. I asked him about my release, given I felt I was truly able to understand my condition now. I asked to stay on temporarily as a farmhand, and was willing to maintain my visits with him. All I wanted was a small stipend for my work, and I assured him I could find a place to stay.

John Hamm had agreed to the plan before I brought it up to the doctor. He had yet to see anything that would make him think I was insane. True, I slept an awful lot in his presence but we had hundreds of mindful conversations that were all sane. He spoke to the doctor on my behalf and a plan was going to be put in motion that I be partially released. I just needed my parents' permission given my young age. I could not be released without it until I was eighteen.

My parents spoke with the doctor and asked to see me. When I was brought before them, it was an emotional meeting. My mother held a newborn baby in her arms, but wouldn't allow me to approach. The child was a boy, as I had suspected. She held him up for me to see and told me his name was Frederick. He was an ugly looking thing with a scrunched up face and oddly shaped forehead. Still, he was my sibling and I felt a yearning to hold him.

"Iona, your hair is growing back nicely. You look well," Father said with sincerity.

"Thank you, Father. I feel well."

"Are they treating you well here?" he asked.

"I have had mostly positive experiences with the staff and yes, my treatment is going well. I like Dr. Macy very much. We have talked about my delusions and I now understand why that was so troubling for you both."

My mother flinched when I said the word "delusions" but my father never batted an eye. He really seemed grateful that I was improving and even though he remained emotionally distant, I felt a slight bit of warmth emanate from him. Mother looked tired and excused herself to nurse the baby.

"Iona, are your visions gone then? Do you still see Hetty? I need to ask before I sign the paperwork and agree to your new arrangement. If you are not fully healed it wouldn't benefit you, or us, to release you partially. And if your treatment is going so well, I suppose I am not sure why I should allow you to move from one bed to another?"

"Well, for one thing, Father, if I am a day patient I can begin controlling my own environment and prepare myself for a future. I can also begin to earn a small stipend for the work I have been doing on a volunteer basis. I am responsible for the stables currently and have pleased the foreman very much."

"I see. It would be nice to think of you down the road, able to care for yourself seeing as you don't have any suitors. The fact that you could save a little money would be nice."

"Yes, well, part of my income would go to pay my rent, but in answer to your previous question, I no longer see Hetty and I feel prepared to leave this place."

"I am glad to hear that. I am worried about releasing you to this Mr. Hamm though because I don't know him. What if he were to take advantage of you?"

"I can assure you that in the seven months I have worked for him he has been the utmost gentleman. I would be a boarder, that is all. I will help with meal preparation and light housework as well. Also, Dr. Macy can vouch for him."

"It still makes me uncomfortable. I will have to discuss this with your mother in private and in the meantime, maybe you can look into other outside arrangements. Isn't there a spinster you could live with until such time as you are fit for release?"

"I don't know, Father, this is the only opportunity that presented itself. Please consider it." I begged my father to allow me this chance to prove I was well. But then, Hetty stood right behind him, picking at her ear-wax and flicking it on the ground. She stomped her right foot impatiently and when I appeared to be looking at her, my father turned his head over his shoulder.

"I was just thinking, Father, there were no visions I assure you." I hadn't seen Hetty in months, so why she appeared now to get me in trouble I didn't understand but I would keep this event to myself and never share it with anyone.

The following day I arrived early at the farm. Pigs from the piggery were being led to the slaughterhouse where their brains would be bashed in leaving the echo of their squeals to ring in my ears for days. I ate breakfast with my fellow workers, forgoing my bacon, and felt a sense of gratitude, for my luck was about to change.

My father needed to discuss things through with my mother but she was overwhelmed and too tired to delve into a lengthy conversation about me. She'd rather brush me aside, happy I was no longer underfoot and seemingly being well taken care of.

I slept a bit, then rode Savannah with James accompanying us on Lucky, a beautiful mount, to give them their exercise. Spring was all around us, flowers were blooming and the ice on the lake had completely thawed. We set up our picnic and as I unwrapped our sandwiches, James leaned in to kiss me as he had many times before. I held to him tightly, wanting the kiss to mean as much to him as it did to me. I had a stirring in my stomach when I was with James; he made me feel giddy and beautiful.

"James," I asked, "do you think my parents will release me to John?"

"I hope so. We'll be under the same roof then and can walk to and from work. Maybe we can even get married one day," he said.

"Get married?" I blushed.

"Well, I am nineteen, and I declare, you make me very happy. I know you are young to be discussing this yet, but if you were home wouldn't you begin courting about now?"

"Why yes, James, I would."

"Well, then, I suppose I would like to start courting you, Iona." He kissed me once more, a deeper, lingering kiss that I felt down to my toes. I knew a kiss such as this would not be permitted in the outside world, but I didn't mind it.

"Does it bother you though, James, that you would court an inmate of the Willard Hospital for the Insane? A woman without proper homemaking skills?"

"I don't think you are insane. You have never shown me that you are anything but stable and strong. Besides that, you are beautiful and a great farmhand. We can muddle through the rest."

"But what if the delusions start again, James, what would you do then?"

"What would you do if I had delusions? Hmm?"

"Why, I would invite them to sit with us for tea, of course."

"Ahhh, then I would do the same."

We kissed a little longer and he lay me down on the blanket. His hand approached my breast and I remembered the way I felt when Cat tried to touch me there. This was different, it was welcome. James stopped his caressing, stood up and claimed he needed to be a gentleman around me. He did not want to take advantage of me, and since I had no one to look out for my well-being, he had to control his impulses better. He also said I needed to resist them, but I didn't want to and if that were a sin so be it.

After our lunch, we rode the beasts farther down the lake, allowing them to gallop and work up a sweat. We had set up logs along the lakeside that they could jump and they did so with little effort, neither breaking their stride. Finally, we slowed the animals to a trot and rode to the farm side by side.

"We could just run away you know. If my father refuses to sign my papers." My voice was as quiet as a whisper.

"I have thought about that, about taking you away from all of this. It wouldn't be an easy life. All I know is farm work and it doesn't pay overly well. I'd rather see if he signs, but if he doesn't, well, we have two beasts that could take us away from here." He gestured with his hands at all that lay around us, what had become my home.

"Giddy up," I said to Savannah, out-pacing Lucky for the jaunt home.

Later in the evening, Patty stormed into my room. "Why you sneaky little whore."

"Patty, please go away." I begged, exhaustion settling into my bones.

"A little birdy told me you were making hay with that farm boy of yours, James, is it? The birdy said you two were rolling all over one another down by the lake today."

"Honestly, Patty, I don't think so."

"Well, I do. Cat is a good little spy and she has told me a few other interesting details as well. I hear you are spending some quality time sleeping in the morning while lover boy mucks the stalls. I suppose you are paying him in interesting ways to do this. I will have to report it at once. This has sin all over it."

"Don't you dare," I spat.

"Afraid, are you? Well, if you don't want it reported I suppose I could try to rid you of the devil myself."

"What do you mean, rid me of the devil? You know what, never mind. Dr. Macy knows how hard I work, he'll never believe you."

"The devil is in you, Iona, it is so strong that it is causing you to sin in the most dreadful of ways, but I know how to rid you of his evil. As for Dr. Macy, if he knew what was going on up in that farm, tsk tsk, he'd be sorry he gave you an opportunity like that. It's no place for a lady anyway, you'll never learn to be a homemaker by working with those beasts. I have a better idea of what needs to be done."

That night Patty entered my room when the lights were out and she tormented me until morning. She violated my body in ways that were previously unimaginable. She shackled my hands and led me to the bathhouse. A tub full to the brim with ice was waiting for me. Patty forced me to disrobe in front of her and then she plunged me into the tub. After nearly an hour in the frigid water, I was certain hypothermia had set in, my teeth chattered nonstop, my skin was blue, and I was numb.

"See there? The red devil is being pulled out, you can get out of the tub now." I could barely rise; the cold air hit me full force and Patty wrapped me in a wet towel.

"I tried starving the beast out of you, now I suppose I'll have to beat it out of you." She launched into a torrent of jabs and punches to my gut. I dropped my towel to protect my body but was too weak and cold from the tub. She never hit my face or arms, only my trunk. She turned me around and punched my kidneys, then started slapping my skin, making it sting as it thawed. Finally, battered and beaten down, she shackled me once more and dragged me, naked, back to my room.

"Take that devil child, Iona." Patty winked at me as she left.

My body could not endure another night like this. My mind could not endure another minute of this. If this was how it felt to be broken, then Patty had succeeded. Still, I forced myself to go through the morning's motions. I showered in cold water because there was no alternative. I dressed in yesterday's attire and ran for the barn. I entered it with red-rimmed eyes and collapsed immediately. Hetty stood beside Savannah, stroking her mane. She glared at me and shook her head in disappointment.

"Shut up, Hetty. Who asked you?"

"Who you talking to, pretty lady?" James had come upon me, bringing hot tea and rolls.

I lay on the ground and sobbed from exhaustion. My body was weak and unmoving.

"James, I cannot bear it. It was awful." I allowed him to cradle me in his lap and comfort me while I replayed the events of the night with disgust.

"I need to leave this place, today. I will not go back there for another night."

"What happened?" James and John were both with me now. I lay propped against James and recounted what took place yesterday, leaving out the most gruesome and shocking of details because they were too humiliating. But because of the way I held my lower stomach, they were able to figure it out.

I told them Patty had a spy and that she found us by the lake and threatened to tell the doctor what was going on, including their involvement. I then told them Patty spent time in my room ridding me of the devil, and left it to their imaginations to determine exactly what I was reduced to. I shivered when recounting the ice bath and beating.

"Why don't you two saddle the horses and take them for some exercise this morning, give me some time to think," John said.

We put blankets under the saddles, included a snack and some water and sauntered away from the barn that had become my safe haven.

"I'm sorry, Iona. It's my fault. I led you to the lake yesterday and kissed you. If Cat saw that, then I am to be held responsible, not you. I will resign from my job and speak to the doctor on your behalf."

"James, can I tell you something?"

"Of course, you can tell me anything."

"Last night, when Patty was beating me, I saw Hetty for the first time in months and now I am afraid. I am crazy, James. Hetty came back to me."

"No, Iona, you were assaulted and it wasn't right. You probably saw stars too. I hope Hetty was able to give you some comfort. God only knows what you went through but I beg your forgiveness." He slowed my horse to a steady gait by pulling on her reins as he rode beside me. He looked all around before leaning in to hug me tight.

"James, I don't know how to say this, but you, you are the only one who has ever cared for me this way. I think I love you, James. Let's run now," I pleaded.

"We could be caught for stealing horses and we don't have any food. Let me gather supplies tonight and we'll run tomorrow. We can go to Waterloo and find jobs. We can sleep in barns until we find proper housing, and when we do, I will make you my wife." I breathed in a sigh of relief.

"Iona, will you be my wife? Will you marry me?"

"In sickness and in health, James?" I had to ask.

"Yes, in sickness and in health."

"Then, yes, I will marry you. Just take me away from this. I never want to look back."

When we returned to the barn we unsaddled and brushed down the horses, then James and John cared for me all afternoon. They dressed the wounds on my wrists as well as the scratches that covered my torso. They were reluctant to allow me to go back to the hospital and tried conjuring stories that would allow me to spend the night at the barn. If only one of the mares was pregnant then they could say they needed a woman to help with the birth. They had to let me go so we didn't arouse any suspicion. We all agreed I had to hang on for one more night, then we would run tomorrow.

Patty came into my room when the lights were out. I lay motionless in bed. My limbs were achy and I had no energy to fight her. She half carried and half dragged me to the ice bath, submerging even my head this time. I wanted to die. I was no match for Patty. If there was such thing as the devil in me, he had surely gone, for I had no fight left. I don't remember being removed from the bath and if I was beaten, I must have passed out. I woke in my bed sometime the next night feeling delirious. My fever was one hundred and five degrees. The nurses were moving me to the sick ward where they could take care of me directly. They would see the bruises and be told I had inflicted them upon myself.

I was diagnosed with influenza. Most patients had come down with it in the winter months but a few patients streamed into the sick ward late in March and early April with fevers and body aches like mine. My glands were swollen to the size of grapes and speaking, eating, or drinking was impossible.

I dreamed of Hetty, sweet, larger than life Hetty. She was brazenly yelling in the ear of the nurse on duty, but when the nurse didn't pay her any attention, I knew I was indeed crazy. I had only one reason to live. James. Hetty tried to nurse me herself, but she couldn't get me to open my mouth to drink and though she tried warming me with her large hands, I shivered for days on end. My fever lasted four days and finally broke the evening of the fifth. I was drenched in sweat and parched. The nurse offered me small sips of water, encouraging me to eat crackers as well. The water slid down my raw throat and landed in my hollow belly, but the crackers were too dry to eat. I stayed in the ward for an entire week. The nurses showed me a kindness I didn't know existed in a mental hospital. They were treating my body, not my mind and therefore weren't concerned with the supposed trouble I caused. They moved me to tears with their gentleness as they swaddled me in blankets and rubbed my hands and feet. They hand-fed me spoonfuls of broth and took time to wash my body and hair. They gently massaged my scalp as they lathered my hair and carefully brushed it out after it was towel dried.

I felt human once more and although I was not restored, I was alive for this one moment and able to refocus my energy. Unfortunately, I was forbidden from working for several days. I was told that I needed to gather my strength before I could I go back. I couldn't imagine what James thought and knew he would be worried about my whereabouts.

Patty had also fallen ill, this was my only saving grace. I still didn't have a blanket to use for warmth, but I was allowed six hours of undisturbed sleep per night. After three days, I was feeling stronger and able to eat small meals. Patty was back with a vengeance on the fourth day. She came immediately to my room, storming in with all her bulk.

"You vile creature, it was you that made me fall ill. The devil's spawn tried to get into me, but I wouldn't let it. You will be rid of it once and for all, Iona. Tonight." She chained me to the bed with my arms spread out to my side. I was mounted in the shape of a cross and left naked. My skin was raw and exposed, goosebumps my only blanket.

I panicked, waves of nausea forced me to vomit my last meal across my naked chest. I shook with apprehension at Patty's threat. She had no empathy whatsoever for me and I knew this would be my last night on earth. I closed my eyes in contemplation. James filled my mind and soul. If I could run to him now I would. If I died right in this moment that would be a saving grace. Just then, my door creaked open and Cat crept into my room.

"She's going to kill you tonight for sure. Here," she said as she fiddled with my restraints, "let me help get you out of here."

"Cat, you loathe me, why on earth would you want to help me now?" I asked through gritted teeth.

"Because you and I are about to run away from this place together. I know what's happening to you, but things are happening to me too. I can't take one more day. You know how to ride a horse, I don't."

I pulled my wrists free and rubbed them to ease the pain. My muscles ached from being stretched and I rolled my shoulders back and forth to loosen them.

"Patty is on her break, it's now or never. Come on," she pulled the pillow out of its case, "grab a few outfits and let's go."

I had no time to think this through but prayed it wasn't a trick. I filled my pillowcase with one set of nightclothes and my shoes, and a skirt and blouse. I would wear my boots and long-johns under another dress. We stood side by side at the door, Cat peered out and when Jay gave her a nod, we snuck down the hallway.

Jay told Cat how to avoid the guards at the building's entrance, so rather than go out the front, we ran to the back of the building, past the main dining hall and lounge and through the laundry room. From there we disposed of our current clothing and put on the white shirts the laundresses wore and, although they were soiled, we didn't care. We donned them anyway and walked straight out in to the night carrying what appeared to be sacks of fresh linen.

Once we made it past the physician's house we were in the clear. A few doctors were still seeing patients, and the night nurses were busy attending them, attendees were on break in the attendee lounge, and only the aides were a concern. We walked across the property when a group of nightshift workers crossed our paths. They were headed to the tin shop. "Ladies," they said, nodding our way, but paying us very little attention. Cat and I breathed simultaneous sighs of relief.

"Cat, I can't just barge into the barn and steal the horses. I have to find James first. He will help us."

"We don't have time for that, Iona. Now go in there and saddle up the pair, I'll wait out here." I walked into the barn but saw no sign of John or James. The stalls were in order, the horses had fresh oats and grain, so someone was here. I couldn't leave without seeing James but he was nowhere to be found.

I saddled Savannah, leaving Lucky behind. Savannah was a steady girl whom I could rely on, while Lucky was a little less predictable at times. I walked her out of the barn, mounted her and pulled Cat up behind me. I tapped Savannah's hindquarters with my boots, urging her into a gallop, and we were off.

CHAPTER EIGHT

ON THE RUN

Cat wasn't nearly as bad as I thought she would be on the run. She didn't make any advances toward me and her attitude was fairly calm. In truth, she did save my life, I owed her that much.

"Where do you think we should go?" Cat asked, putting me in charge that day.

"Well, they'll look for us in Ovid first because it's the closest town. We have to get a good ten miles behind us before anyone realizes we are gone. If we head north along the lake, we will bypass Ovid, go through Romulus and could land in Waterloo. If we head south, we can make it down to Lodi, then Horseheads. I won't go southeast because that would take us through Trumansburg and then Ithaca, where my family lives." I leaned toward Waterloo, remembering the conversation James and I had about possibly living there one day.

"Okay, do we flip a coin or let the horse decide?" Cat asked with a shaky voice.

"Let's not let Savannah decide our destiny. I vote for the north route." I nudged the horse once more in her hindquarters and she began to trot north. We followed the lake's shore, stopping only once to rest Savannah and let her drink her fill. We splashed our faces, went to the bathroom in the tall grass, and ate the stale rolls Cat had snatched and stored in her pillowcase. Perhaps she had been planning this all along. If so, she was brilliant for making Patty think she was out for me. Then again, maybe she still was out for me, I hadn't determined that yet. I still didn't trust her though, she was conniving and narcissistic. I would sleep with one eye open.

"Do you think they know we're gone?" she asked, biting her nails when the sun showed it was past noon.

"Of course they do, and they know Savannah is gone too, she belongs to the doctor. We better get a move on, or they will catch us and we will be arrested and tried for stealing this horse and we'll both become experiments."

Cat fed the horse an apple from her bag and we mounted her once more, riding her all afternoon and into the evening. We stopped for a few hours somewhere along the lake as it grew dark and drank our fill of fresh water. The temperature at night wasn't any worse than what I had grown accustomed to on the ward. We decided to sleep while we could, but as soon as the day broke, we rode Savannah again, trying to make it to a town for a sense of where we were.

As Cat and I ran, my mind drifted to James. He could never love me after this betrayal, although I had left my pair of gloves in the stall so he would know I was there. I hoped he could understand the hidden message, he must know I had no choice but to run.

"Jesus, who are you talking too?" Cat asked.

"Just myself, now shut up." I was trying to pace the horse but worried that if we didn't make it at least to Romulus, we would be found.

Before long, we started seeing other travelers along the roadside. We stopped briefly to give our mare a break, walking her slowly along the edge of the lake. All three of us were tired and hungry. When a group of three men came upon us they slowed down and asked what we were doing out here. We told them we were slightly lost and were following the river back home to Romulus.

"You're getting close then, just another hour or so north, ladies." They tipped their hats at us and left us alone.

When we came upon the small town of Romulus we saw a hotel and a few restaurants. We changed out of our laundress coats into our Sunday dresses before watering Savannah and entering a restaurant. Cat had some change in her pocket; I assumed she stole it but would not ask. The change was enough for breakfast so we sat and ate pancakes. We stuffed ourselves because we didn't know when our next meal would be. We begged an apple for our horse and fed it to her as we left. We tried not to arouse any suspicion, but this was a very small town and folks knew who belonged and who didn't. We told the waitress at the diner that we worked in Ovid, but that we wanted a day of adventure so had taken our horse out for a morning run. She nodded her head as if she believed us but I think she questioned the authenticity of our story. What two young girls would go out riding alone?

After breakfast, we gathered ourselves and continued our journey north, making Waterloo our destination.

"But, Iona, won't they look for us in Waterloo? It's not far enough away, I think we need to keep going," Cat said with determination.

"Maybe we should split up anyway, Cat. They will be looking for two of us and I want to stay put in Waterloo. It's between Cayuga and Seneca Lake and will have lots of farming opportunities for me. I am not sure what you can do for money." I had also held out hope that if James meant his proposal, he would look for me here.

Cat gave a laugh at that and I really didn't want to know her methods of earning a pay day. I had an idea of the favors she would perform for money but didn't want to put any thought into the details.

The weather was simply beautiful, the sun shone off the lake and we were able to enjoy the freedom for a little while as we quietly went about our journey. We talked quite a bit and I learned that Cat was probably as normal a young girl as any, she was definitely more interested in and definitely more knowledgeable than I was about men, and described to me the incident that got her in trouble.

It was Cat's uncle, Samuel, who began courting her when she was a young girl of twelve. She grew to like the attention from him as he always brought her gifts and professed his love to her. Until her father found her in the barn with Sam, who was ten years her senior, she had no idea that simple kisses and touches that brought forth pleasure were considered sinful. She was put on warning and kept locked in the family's attic for weeks. Her mother brought her enough sustenance to keep her alive but while the hours ticked by, Cat grew furious at being jailed in her own home. The night she was allowed out of the attic and back into her room, she snuck out her window and over to her Uncle Samuel's home. She joined him in bed and they became wed in body and spirit. Cat loved this man and found no harm in their activities, but her father found her the next morning and had her admitted to an asylum in Utica for women who were unruly and promiscuous.

"So, you are married?" I asked, slightly confused if there wasn't a wedding or officiate.

"We are, and I promised Sam I would get word to him the moment I escaped from Utica, but as you know that didn't happen. I tried several times, but was caught twice and transferred to Willard for treatment."

"So what about Sam, did he come to look for you?"

"My father threatened his life, but I know Sam, he will be waiting for me. I am sorry by the way, Iona. For treating you so poorly. It was all part of the ruse though, acting tough, getting in with the attendees and so on."

"Yes, but Cat they didn't know what went on behind closed doors, and you came into my bed."

"I said I was sorry, and I won't say it again." She pouted but I was starting to understand her a little more. She wanted to feel loved, as I did, but to her love was physical.

As we rode along the countryside and my belly started to rumble, I contemplated our next meal. I would have to set a few simple snares with a noose and hope to catch some small game. The issue would be starting a fire to cook it.

When Savannah grew too tired to carry our weight, we leapt off and walked beside her. We settled in an area densely populated with trees and shrubs to stay the night. I searched the grounds for small game trails, which usually led from the water to their shelter. I sought tracks, and scat, along with tracks, rubs, and burrow entrances. I found rabbit scat and tracked it to the hole in the ground that I presumed was the burrow. Now I needed a cattail to make a noose, along with two sticks with "Y" shaped nooks. Luckily for me, several small trees and branches were in the ground in line with the entrance to the burrow. I took off my boots and long underwear and waded into the water's edge where it was slightly swampy and the cattails grew. I could feel the grass between my toes as I sunk into the soft earth. I grabbed a few stalks and began my work of making nooses. I showed Cat how to do it so we could have several traps set for the night. We worked side by side, attaching the lead and weighting it with a rock, then draped the noose at the entrance and went to lay down. When we heard a movement, we rushed to the trap and sure enough, we had a rabbit. She was only a few pounds but that was enough for a meal. I snapped her neck, and began ripping at her belly.

"Stop," Cat uttered.

"Cat, if you don't want to watch look away."

"No, wait, I have a knife." She produced a knife meant for buttering bread and rolls but it was better than using my fingers to part the fur and flesh of the animal, which was till was warm in my hands.

I gutted the animal, threw the entrails in the woods, and skinned it in preparation to cook. We worked on a primitive fire by collecting brush and dried leaves, then rubbing two rocks together. After an hour or more, we had a spark, and luckily, it caught on a leaf, I blew gently on the smoke and the fire indeed spread. We constructed a spit and placed the rabbit on top. In a short time, it was cooked well enough for us to eat. We each had a leg, and split the rest evenly.

"I can't believe you know how to do that."

"Yes, well, it is part of the reason my parents thought I was insane. I preferred to be outdoors honing skills such as these than indoors sewing for my dowry. I was disobedient and my refusal to participate in activities meant for ladies made my folks distraught. When my mother became pregnant, they sent me away." I left out the part about my delusions, hoping this was enough to satisfy her curiosity for now.

"I am grateful you had this skill or we'd be starving. Let's dampen the fire and maybe get a little farther down the pathway. I feel a little strange right here for some reason," she said, looking around, obviously feeling paranoid.

Cat's premonition was not far off, for in a few hours we heard men on horseback ride past us about one hundred yards away. We had positioned Savannah behind a massive oak tree and remained quiet until they were gone. We didn't know if they were looking for us or were out with another search party. Either way, our movement forward was in jeopardy.

When we arrived in Waterloo, we were both feeling unwell. Cat was feverish and rail thin, while I was nauseous and unable to keep food down. I had thrown up several times and had to stop to huddle in the bushes while my insides exploded. My nerves had gotten the best of me. We washed in the lake so, at the very least, we were presentable. Cat had one dollar and thirty cents left and I had one quarter. We walked inside the first hotel we saw and presented ourselves to the clerk as Savannah and Sylvia Woods, two sisters from Syracuse.

The clerk took all our change and gave us the key to a room; it was sparse, but it had a bed and tub. Mealtime was in an hour so, we had that long to relax and settle down for a moment before toasting our success. I filled the tub with warm water and tested it with my big toe. It was ideal, so I submerged myself and closed my eyes. Hydrotherapy did in fact relax my muscles and mind at the same time and I relished this moment. I emptied the tub and refilled it for Cat, who was sleeping soundly on the bed.

"Cat, wake up, I've drawn you a bath." Cat woke up, but the violet circles beneath her eyes and goose bumps on her arms told me she was not well. I helped her into the tub and handed her the soap the hotel provided.

"No offense, but you stink." We both chuckled.

"Iona, I just need to rest, you go down to supper, okay? Maybe bring me back something."

I brushed my hair with my fingers and shook out my clothes from my pillowcase. My dress was dull and unassuming, ensuring I would not stand out. When the clerk saw me enter the hotel's lounge, he waved me over.

"Did you say your name is Savannah?" he asked.

"Why yes I did, why?" I panicked.

"I have a note here in case a Savannah should check in. It's from a gentleman named James. He is staying at the hotel down the street. Here is the address." He handed me a small piece of paper, but before I could even look at it, I ran down the street in search of James. He knew me all too well, as I had hoped. I found him with Lucky outside the hotel tavern where he was staying.

"James!" I yelled, running to him. He turned toward me and dropped Lucky's reins. He watched as I ran toward him, and held his arms open for me to crumble in.

"Iona, thank God. I prayed for days that you were still alive. I knew you could manage with snares but worried you'd be caught. Do you know how many search parties are out for you?"

"I don't care. They won't find us now, will they?"

"They might. Half of the men went south toward Watkins Glen and the other half were split in pairs and sent to Trumansburg and Ithaca, as well as across to Cayuga Lake. Apparently another patient is missing too, someone named Kate."

"Yes, Cat, she is with me. I owe her my life, James. Patty would have killed me if I were there even one more night." I sobbed into James's arms, feeling the magnitude of the situation. I was a moment shy of death and Cat changed that. James kissed my tears and together we walked toward Lucky. We hitched him to a post and went up to the room James had procured at the hotel.

"Sit." James pointed to the edge of the bed. "Now, tell me everything."

I recounted the torture of the ice baths, the beatings, the chaining and threats. I told him the personal ways in which my body was abused as well. Then I told him I nearly died. I told him Hetty was there trying to care for me but she couldn't because she wasn't real. The nurses were the ones I credit for my health today. If not for their kindness and concern I would surely have died. James pulled me close to him and we cried together for a long time.

"I was worried sick about you. The staff would not let me see you as a visitor, nor would they let John. They told us you were dreadfully sick and that you might not make it. They said you were covered in bruises and gashes that you inflicted upon yourself during one of your episodes, but I knew it was Patty. I waited for her after her shift ended one night and cornered her so that she had no possibility of escape. I swear, Iona, I felt mad, like I could have killed that woman. She told me you had the flu, that she had bathed you to bring down your fever. She promised to put me on the visitation list the next day, but by then you had run."

"We had no choice. Cat knew Patty meant to kill me and she was in trouble too."

"I thought she was intolerable. How has she been?"

"She's been okay. I understand her now, what she has been through and why she does what she does. She is under the weather now, I need to tend to her but I don't want to leave you again, James, ever."

"I'll come with you. Let's eat a meal first and we'll go see to her together."

We walked hand in hand toward my hotel, we ate heartily, and went upstairs, only to find Cat missing. A note was sprawled across the tabletop for me, reading:

Iona, my friend and fellow lunatic,
    I think we should separate now so that they don't find us. I am going after Samuel. Wish me luck. I have taken the horse.
Cat

"Oh my, she'll never make it when she is this sick." I told James about Samuel and together we prayed that someone was looking out for Cat and that she would find her happily-ever-after.

James turned to me and asked, "What about our happily-ever-after? "How about we get married?"

"Right now?" I asked.

"Yes, I want you by my side tonight and forever more."

"James, are you really here? I have to be sure I am not imagining this, pinch me."

Obligingly, James pinched me under my arm and sure enough, I felt it. I hugged him once more and we left in search of a priest to marry us.

CHAPTER NINE

MARRIAGE

James and I decided to make Waterloo our home. We were married immediately by a justice of the peace whom the hotel manager helped us locate. Our first night together as man and wife was unremarkable. I was so exhausted from my escape that,while we shared a marriage bed, my good husband simply carried me across the doorway of our hotel room and settled me into a nest of covers. I lay safely beside him and slept for nearly fifteen hours.

When I woke, James was waiting for me. I bathed alone, soaping my private areas and armpits, then my stinky feet. I wrapped myself in a towel and when I came out from the bathroom, I opened it like a gift before my husband. He had never seen a naked woman before and dropped to his knees before me, appraising me and taking my offering. Hugging his head to my belly and caressing me with gentle touches, I relaxed in his arms. His soft lips took my mouth and he explored the cavern with his tongue. His kisses were gentle but there was a neediness I understood. We fell onto the bed and clumsily learned about one another. The contours of my lover's body were that of a man who worked hard. His arms were muscular and his chest well defined. He said I was far too skinny and that he had every intention of fattening me up. We made sweet and satisfying love to one another that morning, that afternoon, and again that night. We only left our room for meals, it was our honeymoon after all and we were two lovebirds with much to celebrate.

"James, what shall we do today?" I asked after our second day sequestered in our room.

"We will tend to Lucky and find a place of our own to live," he said, as he rubbed his hands through my growing hair.

"James, did you steal Lucky?" I had to ask.

"No, I wouldn't say that. They owe me an awful lot of back pay, Iona, so I felt at liberty to take him in exchange."

We purchased a newspaper for a penny and looked at the employment sections for work, as well as the real estate section for homes. James found several jobs that looked intriguing and left me to go speak with managers and foremen at different locations. I continued to comb the paper, but didn't find anything suitable for my skills. There were plenty of jobs for seamstresses and laundry maids, there were even opportunities for caregivers, but until I saw the opening at the bait and tackle shop I was not intrigued. I walked to the shop and noted the "help wanted" sign in the window. I took a deep breath to calm my nerves before entering.

An older man behind the counter asked, "Can I help you, miss?"

"I am here about the job," I stuttered.

"Oh no, I can't hire a woman, ain't nobody would take you seriously. They'd be thinking they could pull one over on ya and take advantage. Nope, go on now, I can't hire you." He showed me out the door, dismissing me immediately. Hetty walked right beside me, chatting about how unfair that was. "We'll keep looking, yes we will. I taught you to clean, you could do that." Hetty was well intentioned but I didn't want to clean tubs for a living. I had too many bad memories associated with them now. I walked through the small town, counting paces while taking in the sights, smells, and sounds of my new surroundings. I was careful not to arouse suspicion by conversing with Hetty lest people think I was crazy and start gossiping about me. When she talked, I listened but didn't respond. This irked her but she understood why I was behaving this way; she didn't want me back at Willard any more than I did. I duly noted that she was an apparition now and accepted her presence.

James and I met back at the hotel. We ate quickly, then ran to our room to make love before he started his first job. He was lucky, someone at the mill up and quit a few days earlier and they were looking for anyone who could start right away. He didn't have a recommendation but they could tell he was a hard worker by one look at his body.

"I can't believe I start right away. The first few days are just a trial, but I want you to start looking for a house, or land anyway. Maybe we can build our own place. I have some money saved from years of work. John never let me pay him rent so I saved and saved. I have just about three thousand dollars. I would have had more if they paid me my wages for the past two months, but the hospital was struggling."

"I will start looking when you leave, or maybe I'll just lay here a while and wait for you to come back, don't be too long now." I looked at him provocatively, loving the way we were able to make one another feel. I didn't want him gone from me for one single minute.

I decided to start with the desk manager. I asked if he knew of any properties or any land that was for sale. He didn't, but would put the word out. I strolled through town, looking at notices hanging in windows at the grocer's and baker's. I found one alluring sign; it described an older, charming home a few miles outside of town. The property was close to water and had ten acres. I grew up with an enormous amount of land and this was nowhere near that, but we could keep some animals and livestock if we wanted. I guessed charming meant the house needed work, and maybe we would prefer to start fresh, but still it was worth considering. I got directions from the bakery owner and since I had nothing else to do, I walked to the property. I knocked on the door but no one answered. I decided to have a look around anyway. The property itself was overgrown and had been left deserted for a long time, but it held great promise. The home had a nice structure and after peering in the windows, seemed decent in size.

I was entrusted with James's money. I took a five dollar bill and went into a few stores to purchase some necessary items. I bought a frying pan, a saucepan, and a spatula and wooden spoon. I would need a few towels and oven-mitts, so I bought those too. I had the items wrapped in parcel paper and waited patiently for James, who didn't arrive home until after the dinner hour. I was growing fearful something awful happened to him, but when he came in and removed his hat, I realized just how hard he worked today and forgave him for the scare. He bathed and ate, then fell fast asleep before I could present him with the gifts. The following morning we rose together and I brought the packages to him.

"What are these?" he asked, befuddled.

"Just a little something for our new home."

He unwrapped the items and swept me up into his arms. "They'll be perfect, did you find us a place then?" he asked, amused.

"I haven't spoken with the owners, but I have seen the property and it will do just fine."

"I have tomorrow off, let's go look at it then. I can hardly wait, but for now, I must be off to the mill. Enjoy yourself today."

It turned out the property owners were deceased and a distant relative was selling the homestead. He wanted far more than the property was worth and we weren't willing to part with our entire nest egg. After bickering back and forth between lawyers, we obtained the property for two thousand and four hundred dollars. The lawyer also had a fee, so after we paid him, we were left with about five hundred dollars to our name. It wasn't much, but for us all that mattered was having a place to call home.

On his days off, James cleared the property and repaired the stables while I took care of the inside of the house. It had been well kept and still had some furnishings that we gladly used. The oak kitchen table sat four people, so I envisioned my husband and me and our two children all eating meals together there. I wiped it down and oiled it, then set to work on the floors. I swept and mopped, then dusted the cobwebs that lingered in the cupboards. I saw a few vermin scatter across the floor and jumped onto the kitchen chair, screaming for James. When he came in, he had an expression of terror, but when he saw me with a broom and up off the floor he guessed we had mice. His laughter filled the house, making me love him and this place, our place, even more.

"Once we really get settled in here the mice will move out. Until then, don't go anywhere without your broom," he said, laughing. He got a tall glass of water and then went back to do more yard work. He said he had a surprise for me and he was trying to finish it before dusk.

I prepared a measly dinner of pancakes and eggs. I didn't know how to cook very well and this would have to do for now. After we ate, James took my hand and led me outside. He had me close my eyes and when I opened them, before me was a chicken coop. My very own coop. It was nicely constructed and just the perfect size.

"Oh, James, you remembered. Thank you. Now we have to get some chickens!"

"My boss at the mill said we can go to his place tomorrow, he has more than he needs now that it's just he and his wife. She'd like to meet you as well and help you get acquainted to the area, so the official invite is for dinner. Is that okay with you?"

"Of course, I'd be delighted to meet them. It is a very kind invitation, but what shall I wear? I only have the two skirts…"

"Take a few dollars, go into town and buy a nice outfit. Buy me one too!"

I bought us both some much-needed new clothes and a pie from the bakery so we didn't arrive empty handed. I was letting my nerves get the better of me. What if they found out who we really were? Or what if they pried into our background and asked how we met? I would need a convincing story. We were pretty young comparatively to be married and living on our own already.

James came home to freshen up and we were off to dinner. The couple were Ben and Jennifer Mills. They looked to be in their late forties and had several children who had moved on to larger cities, leaving them alone with the mill.

"Your home is just lovely, Jennifer," I said, remembering my manners.

"Thank you, do come in and have a proper look around." It was a very inviting home, fluffy lace pillows adorned the davenport, hand-hooked rugs covered nearly all the wooden floors. Watercolor paintings lined the side tables and walls.

I felt so lacking in my ability to make a home and said as much to Jennifer. To my surprise, she offered to help me spruce our place up. I admitted I was not much of a sewer or cook for that matter and she grew slightly apprehensive for a moment. I told her James and I were young lovers and that we ran from home to be together. I begged that she not tell anyone. It explained how we arrived in a new town without any family waiting for us, or helping us. It didn't explain why I was so deficient in womanly ways. I added that my mother lacked the patience to teach me, and that because there were so many mouths to feed at my house, it was easier to send me outside, which was the reason I was so good with animals.

Jennifer understood and didn't ask further questions. She served us an impressive meal of pork chops smothered in apple butter, alongside a vegetable casserole, and hot buttered rolls. It was delicious, and had me wondering where she found the time. I supposed she prepared the crusts for the casserole and the rolls earlier in the day and realized I would soon be doing the same if I were to take care of a family. My time would be spent in the house more often than not and I wasn't quite comfortable with that.

That night I told James my concerns that he wouldn't love me if I couldn't cook properly or take care of the home sufficiently. He promised to help and I held him to his word.

We had come home with not two or three, but five chickens for our coop. We had fresh hay that I scattered around and a trough full of grains for feeding. I sat in the coop with the girls and closed my eyes, remembering back to when I was a young girl collecting eggs. I wondered about my family. I ruminated about my new baby brother, Frederick, and how they were all getting along. I shook off the image and gathered myself before heading indoors.

James worked long, arduous hours. I was often left home alone from sunup to sundown. Luckily, Jennifer paid me frequent visits, sensing my loneliness. On one such occasion, she brought with her two fluffy pillows that she had made, but no longer required and settled them on the davenport. She looked at our lackluster decor and suggested we go shopping.

"I know just the place." She grabbed my hand like we were old friends and together we marched into town. There were several stores I hadn't noticed before that had all kinds of knick-knacks. I was disinclined to spend too much money, but did buy a few little items to make my place homier. I bought a pair of salt and pepper shakers in the shape of chicks, and a cuckoo clock to go over the mantle. I had spent my limit, but then I saw the baby blanket. It was a velvety soft, light blue blanket with a lace pattern. I grabbed it and held it to my cheek, then marched to the counter and checked out with all of my items.

When I returned home, I hung the clock and filled the shakers before placing them in the center of the oak table. Combined with the pillows, things were looking more like a home. I tucked the baby blanket into my closet, behind my clothing so James couldn't see it.

Every night I waited for my husband to come home, but more often, I ate and fell asleep before he walked through the door. He put his earnings on the counter and climbed into bed beside me, sometimes without eating. He was overworked, but never complained. The pay was good and we would be able to save for a family this way. I only minded when he was too tired to bed me. I looked forward to our intimate moments all day long, sometimes bathing right before he was due home so I would smell enticing.

Weeks went on this way and I started spending more time with Jennifer. She invited me to a sewing club, but I declined. I was far too ashamed by my skills to join a club of ladies who were sure to be advanced. Jennifer offered to come to my house once a week for a few hours to sew with me, she didn't mind what my skill level was, she just wanted the company, she said.

So every Tuesday at ten a.m., Jennifer arrived with sweets and her sewing basket. I had to pull out my pillowcases that I was embroidering and pretend to enjoy myself. Hetty stood behind Jennifer and belly laughed.

"Is someone behind me?" Jennifer asked one day.

"Oh, no, I was just thinking of my old friend, Hetty. She always tried to get me to sew. If she could see me now!" I laughed. Then I thought about sewing with my mother, she always grew impatient and frustrated with me, whereas Jennifer had the patience of a saint. We laughed at my mistakes and didn't seek perfection.

"You're coming along fine, all you need is practice. Now, what are you serving your husband for supper tonight?"

"I hadn't thought about it yet. Usually we have eggs and biscuits, or a slab of ham and some pancakes."

"Let's put the sewing down and bake a nice pie. I brought some fresh berries from our bushes. Ben and I can't eat them all before they go bad, so I hoped maybe you'd like them."

"How kind. I would love to make a pie, but honestly, Jennifer, I don't know how."

"I am here to teach you. The crust is the hardest part, but if you can make biscuits, you can make pie crust."

So our first cooking lesson began. I cut the cold-pressed lard into the flour mixture as explained to me and then mixed it into a large lump. Then I rolled it out to create a nice symmetrical circle. I laid the dough out into a pan and cut the edges off so they didn't hang over and burn when cooking. Then I filled it with a mixture of fresh berries we had let stew with sugar. The leftover dough was used to make lattice-work on top of the pie. We baked it for forty minutes and put it on the windowsill to cool. I was proud of the accomplishment and couldn't wait to show James. However when he came home, it was one of the evenings he was too tired to eat, think, talk, or bed me.

That night I ate the pie directly from the pan with a fork, not cutting slices but starting in the center and working my way out. I felt nauseous all the next day and wondered if it was my cooking. My brow sweated and I had to sit down a few times. I felt better as the afternoon passed, but the following morning after I ate, I felt like I would vomit.

The week passed and as Tuesday arrived, I dreaded visiting with Jennifer. She could when she came through my doorway that something was wrong.

"Iona, is it possible you could be pregnant?" We were seated together on the couch.

"Oh my goodness, I suppose!" I laughed and jumped up from my seated position, grabbing Jennifer's hands and circling the room with her in a dance.

She hugged me and offered her congratulations. We figured I was still early in my pregnancy and that I should keep it a secret a little longer in case it didn't take. She promised to show me a few other recipes that I could make easily and quickly with little ones in tow and then she pulled out two skeins of yarn from her infamous, bottomless, basket. Next, she pulled out two wooden needles.

"Let's teach you to knit so we can make booties and sweaters and hats for the little one. It's so exciting."

It was exciting, but terrifying as well. I didn't have a good relationship with my mother and hardly knew how to be a mother. I couldn't focus on Jennifer's instructions on how to knit and purl.

"You're scowling. What is it?" Jennifer asked.

"I just want to be a good mother, that's all."

"Well, you're a good wife, so you'll be a good mother too!" She had no doubt at all that I would do fine.

"I suppose." Hetty held the scowl now and later, when my guest left, I would find out why.

My nausea came in waves. By night, I felt better, but in the mornings I was unable to keep any food down. I was bone tired all day long and spent most of my time in bed. When James came home that evening, I was still slumbering.

"Iona?" he called.

I stirred and suddenly jolted from bed; I had nothing prepared for supper, as my husband was rarely home at this hour.

"Are you sick? You look a little peaked."

"You could say that."

"Is that a riddle? You are either sick or you're not, which is it?" He was slightly crabby, which wasn't unusual lately.

"James, sit. I have news." I couldn't keep this from him. I was terrible at keeping secrets.

My husband pulled out a chair and sat with his elbows on the table.

"What is it, Iona, you're scaring me."

"You're about to be a father, you should be scared!"

"What?" His expression changed from one of surprise to terror, then to elation. He swept me off my feet and kissed me on the lips.

"Really, are you certain? We're having a baby?" He put his hands protectively across my flat belly and grimaced.

"It's early yet, just wait, he'll be kicking in no time."

"I am just so happy, our own little family. Gosh, we are doing it, aren't we?"

"Making our way? Yes, we are, but James, I admit I am afraid. I don't know how to be a mother. I can barely cook for you and me, let alone keep up our home. I am afraid you won't love me the same if I can't do it all."

"You're giving me a child, what is better than that? I can help cook and clean and I'll tell Ben I need shorter hours once he or she arrives. Until then, maybe I should double up and save extra money. What do you think?"

"I think it gets lonely here all day without you."

"I know. Ben is apprenticing me so I can take over one day. He won't work forever and his children are not interested in millwork. It could be ours one day to run and operate; it would secure our future so that we can buy a nicer house and have all kinds of special things for our family."

"James, I don't need any of that. I grew up in a fancy house with all the trimmings and look where it got me."

My home may have had a lot of fancy furnishings and finery, but it was sterile and dry. The irony that my mother told me dozens of times that "one day I'd be sorry if I didn't learn to stitch and knit, sew and cook" hit me with full force now. I was indeed sorry I hadn't learned these skills, yet at the same time I still didn't want to learn them. I wanted this child, and to be a mother, but did that mean I had to become a slave to the household?

CHAPTER TEN

LUCY

Lucy was born seven and a half months later. The contractions started slowly at first, but when my water broke at four in the morning, the pain left me breathless. James was sound asleep besides me, but I was tossing and turning all night long with the feeling of indigestion. When I could no longer bear the intense cramping, I tapped James on the shoulder to wake him. He was startled upon seeing my discomfort, but jumped to action. He knew his first order of business was to get Jennifer and the midwife.

I was fine alone for the hour it took him to gather the women. I paced the well-worn floors holding tight to my belly. I took small sips of water and wiped my sweating brow. All the while, I prayed for an easy delivery. The midwife had come to check me several times throughout my pregnancy and she declared that my hips were made for birthing. I wasn't so sure I agreed. The labor put extra pressure on my pelvis, making me feel that I had to relieve myself. I had an urge to push but promised I would wait for help. In moments, the door flew open and the ladies came in. They assessed the situation and began getting my bed ready for the birth. James came to my side, but was sent into the kitchen to boil water and make tea.

"I need to push, Kathy," I told the midwife.

"Let me check you first." She knelt down between my legs and agreed the baby was coming quickly. Its head was already visible, so she told me to push. I pushed three times and the baby's head was out, followed by the rest of her. Her cries echoed in my bedroom and nothing could keep James from entering. He came in the room and went straight to his daughter, counting her fingers and toes. Then he smiled at me with newfound amazement. He kissed his baby on her forehead and then kissed me. The women gathered the birthing sheets and mopped the floor, before giving us our first moments alone as a family.

"She is beautiful, just like her mother," James said.

"Are you disappointed, James?" I asked because it was a girl and not a boy as I hoped.

"How could I be? She is lovely. What shall we name her?"

"I like Lucy. What do you think?"

"Lucy it is then."

Kathy came back into the room with fresh towels for me to expel the afterbirth. Then she taught me to nurse. She had me cradle the baby's head in alignment with my breast and nipple. Lucy latched on lazily and kept slipping. I had to hold my nipple in her mouth and express milk until she latched on firmly and could extract the sustenance on her own. Once she learned how to nurse, she became an expert.

James took the ladies home when they were certain everyone was healthy. After they left, I dozed on and off with Lucy beside me. I would keep the blue baby blanket tucked away in the closet for our next little one. I felt a sense of pride and accomplishment when I stared down at my sleeping beauty. Her tiny fingers latched onto my own and the feeling caused my milk to let down. I put her to my breast, but she was too tired and full to want to bother with feeding. I held her and nodded off. I only woke when James crept back into the bed, cradling the baby between us, safe and sound.

She woke urgently a few hours later, crying to be fed. I was happy enough to nurse her although exhaustion was setting in and my woman's parts were tender. I put her to my right breast and then alternated to the left, but she kept falling asleep in between. She never got her fill; instead she became a constant snacker. I was unable to do much else, so her chronic nursing didn't bother me.

"Hello, darling girl. You are beautiful, yes you are." I cooed, picking up my darling girl, breathing her in and kissing her forehead. I unclothed and bathed her with a washcloth and warm water in the sink and noted how she startled when the water trickled down her belly. She enjoyed her bath and even opened her eyes wide enough to investigate me.

Hetty reached out to hold her, but I told her no. I continued with the bath before drying and then swaddling my little girl. I was told that most babies sleep a lot, but Lucy had other ideas. She catnapped for ten minutes here or there, but never for long stretches. After a week of constant feedings and very little sleep, I was ready to collapse. My nipples were cracked and bleeding, and there was searing pain when Lucy latched on. I developed the chills and James called Kathy to come check on me at once. She assessed the situation and diagnosed me with mastitis on both breasts. The baby would need to have an alternate way of feeding while I healed. We wrapped my breasts in cabbage leaves and changed them every two hours in order to draw out the infection. We tried glass bottles with Lucy, and while she was reluctant at first, after several tries she finally accepted the fake nipple and drank a few ounces.

I admit I felt relieved when she took the bottle from James, and I prayed that tonight he would give our daughter her night-time feedings so that I might sleep solidly for a few hours. I hardly heard her cries, but felt James climb out of bed to prepare the bottle for Lucy. I drifted back to sleep and didn't wake again until morning and by then Jennifer had arrived to help. She fed the baby all day long and insisted I stay put in bed. She filled the bath for me and brought me more cabbage leaves for my breasts. Lucy was very content and I felt so much better as the day progressed.

I watched my friend as she comforted my baby. Her movements were natural and calm. I was in awe at how easily nurturing a baby was for her. I felt awkward and questioned all of my movements. I was tired and cried often now as a result. I wasn't myself and didn't know if I ever would be again.

My body healed and I was physically capable of caring for my child. Lucy was quite needy and cried more than she rested. Jennifer called it "colic" and claimed one of her boys had it too. Colicky babies were fussy and hard to soothe, she explained, but it got better with time, she assured me. I tried holding Lucy with her belly positioned against my arm. I rocked her, walked her, and sometimes just let her cry herself to sleep. I was at my wit's end by the afternoon. Preparing supper was nearly impossible with a baby who required so much attention. Still, I tried to at least scramble eggs or make toast.

James didn't complain about our small meals. He took the baby when he came home at night and ordered me to sit, or go outdoors to be alone. He sensed my frustration and felt it as well when Lucy was having one of her fits. She also spit up continuously so we wondered if she was digesting the milk we provided, and if she was always hungry.

One afternoon when I had tried everything to appease my daughter, I felt so frustrated that I needed to leave her or I was afraid I would hurt her. I left her in the center of the bed, entombed among the pillows that I propped all around her so she wouldn't fall off. I wasn't afraid she would roll over, she was far from that, I was only concerned she would throw up and choke. Still, I had to get away. I went into the chicken coop and covered my ears to muffle the sound of her cries. I put a chicken on my lap and began plucking her feathers, she tried to get away and clucked at my shoulder with her beak, but I held her down. Once the cries stopped and silence ensued, I let the bird go. Suddenly I was terrified something was wrong so I ran to the house, but Lucy was sleeping peacefully. She woke fifteen minutes later with red-rimmed eyes from crying so much. I picked her up and apologized for leaving her.

"Lucy, I love you, darling. It is hard though, please understand and don't be mad." I rocked her and kissed her cheeks.

When she was a few months old, Jennifer suggested that we try solid foods. So we mixed powdered rice with milk to a thin consistency she could handle. She turned her nose up at first, but finally started to eat. She soon gained a small amount of weight and slept better at night.

I had developed insomnia and found sleep elusive. At night, I paced the floors while James and Lucy snuggled together and slept. I worried about my daughter's health and her tiny weight. I was afraid I would do something wrong, like lay her the wrong way or drop her. Jennifer told me it was normal to fret, that it meant I was a good mother. My anxiety peaked and I became obsessed with Lucy's care and the orderliness of the house. I drove myself crazy by seeking perfection.

Hetty and I cleaned the tub together, making it appear spotless. We scrubbed the floors and dusted the furniture every day. When the baby cried, I instinctively tended to her needs, but whenever I held her, I felt unease because of all the laundry that was piling up, or the barn that needed fresh hay, or the bed that had to be made.

I drove myself crazy until one day Lucy rolled over and smiled up at me. I was overcome with joy. I felt an acceptance by her in that moment that melted my heart. I cheered her as she rolled again and again. She cooed and smiled, recognizing her feat and sensing my enthusiasm.

I could hardly wait to tell James when he came home that night. For once, I left the chores and just played with my baby. It was delightful, her smile was bright and contagious. We lay together on the rug and rolled left and right, holding each other's hands, staring into one another's eyes and bonding, finally. All those months of colic made me feel inferior; nothing I tried helped ease my child's discomfort. Today, however, was a new beginning.

CHAPTER ELEVEN

LUCY AND SUZETTE

"Look at her go," James said.

Lucy had taken her first steps between James and me unexpectedly one Saturday afternoon. We were outdoors by the water's edge, enjoying a picnic of chicken and biscuits. I held Lucy in an upright position and she attempted to toddle forward but quickly fell. We picked her up and she tried again, soon enough she took two, then three steps between us. After a week of toddling, she was an expert walker and had so much to explore. She didn't like to be too far away from me, but would dare to go in the parlor while I was in the kitchen, calling for me, "ma?" while she discovered new things.

She said "ma-ma" and "da-da" and recognized us as the recipients to her words. She said "ba-ba" too and learned to point at her bottles on the counter when she was hungry.

"It's such a relief, James," I said one night, appreciating the fact that Lucy slept soundly through the night now and no longer lay between James and me.

"I agree," James said, as he slowly undressed me and began bedding me once more. He brought me to pleasures I hadn't known were possible, but we always muffled our voices, because we didn't want to be interrupted by a crying infant.

"I love you, James," I said, gazing into his knowing eyes.

"I love you more," he chimed in, kissing my nose.

James cut back on his hours a few days a week in order to lend a hand around the house. We ate together as a family and put the baby to bed soon after so we could enjoy quality time together.

All of the bedding led to a second pregnancy. Lucy would be having a sibling within the year. I was certain I was carrying again, and when I told my husband he was thrilled to add to our family. I enjoyed the thickness of my belly the second time around, and appreciated each little flutter and kick. This baby was larger, and my appetite was heartier. I was also more tired, so certain jobs like dusting went undone. I tried not to fret over the house and instead allowed myself a reprieve. I occasionally had anxious moments when the toilet was growing brown with stains, or we had eaten eggs for three nights in a row.

On one such occasion, I slaughtered one of our chickens and prepared it for our evening meal. I de-boned the bird so it would fit in our small oven, seasoned the skin with salt and pepper and put it in early to bake slowly so it would be nice and succulent. I chopped carrots and made a pie, all while Lucy napped. I felt so accomplished in this moment and knew I was a good mother.

That night, I felt as if I had it all. My husband was delighted to have such a hearty meal, my daughter was healthy, and I felt certain I was carrying a boy. I had made one friend, Jennifer, and rarely thought of my time at Willard, of Cat, or of my family and siblings. I had my own family now and took joy in each fragile moment.

Four months later, my water broke. I felt the soaked sheets beneath me in bed as I slept and woke thinking I had peed myself. I knew, however, that this was different, because the labor pains began almost immediately.

"James, James, wake up." I shook him awake frantically for I was not due for two more months.

"What is it, what time is it?"

"It's the middle of the night, but, James, my water broke. You need to get Kathy and Jennifer."

My husband pulled on a shirt and pants, then ran out the door to fetch help. We were both fearful, because it was early.

"Push!" Kathy ordered, while Jennifer held tight to my hand.

"It's a girl!" she announced, after an hour of hard labor.

"How is she, Kathy? Is she going to be okay?" We were all worried what it meant that she was premature, but Kathy said based on her color and wail that she was healthy even if she was on the small size. She suggested keeping her in a warming pan while she slept as a precaution.

We named her Suzette Grace and we adored her from the moment she entered our lives.

"She is so different from Lucy," James said, as when we lay in bed side by side a few nights after her birth.

"She is a fighter. She nurses well, sleeps well and doesn't fuss," I added.

"Thank God. I am not sure I could handle another colicky baby," my husband admitted.

"Thank God is right, she is certainly good natured, and Lucy is precious with her." Our sweet little family was perfect. I wanted so badly to give my husband a son, but for now, we had these two darling angels. I got up and grabbed the blue baby blanket I had saved for nearly two years and presented it to James.

"I was hoping to give this to you if it was a boy."

"It's so soft, why can't we use it anyway? We'll have a boy next." I agreed there would be a next time because I loved our family so dearly. My husband was attentive to the girls and to me as well. He always kissed me first when he came in from work, and he provided well for us. I was growing to enjoy being a homemaker and saw no reason not to expand.

❖

After a few weeks of bliss, I started to feel exceedingly tired and melancholy. Jennifer called it the "baby blues" and said it would go away in time. She suggested I nurse for as long as I could to help balance my hormones. Suzette felt extraordinarily heavy in my arms and I always wanted to sleep. I often fell asleep when the girls were awake, but my body needed the rest so desperately that I relented and just lay down on the couch. I slacked off when it came to meal preparation and settled on toast for dinners. Over the course of a few weeks, the house was disorderly and disheveled.

"James, I just can't muster the energy to do it all," I said apologetically one night.

"The house doesn't have to be perfect, Iona, as long as the children are healthy, that's all that matters." I wouldn't admit to him that I often napped throughout the day. I was beginning to feel like a failure but didn't have the wherewithal to change.

The following night when James came home, he made dinner and took care of the girls. I lay on the couch and closed my eyes. Three weeks ago, life was perfect, how had I unraveled in such a short period of time? I was irritable and impatient with Lucy, and didn't have the desire to nurse Suzette. She would nurse around the clock if I let her but I kept her to a schedule of every three hours so I could have a reprieve. She was gaining weight and all signs pointed that she was normal and healthy.

"We have so much to be grateful for, James. So why don't I feel happy anymore?" I cried as he held me one night.

"Honey, everything will be fine. Trust me. You just need more rest, the girls take so much out of you and it's taxing on your body."

My body was rail thin, I lost the baby weight very quickly this time. That night, James tucked the children snug in bed and we fell asleep together as usual.

"What are you doing? It's two in the morning." James chided me when he found me awake and working in the kitchen.

I felt like I was in a trance. Hetty woke me up to do some proper cleaning and I followed her into the kitchen. We started with polishing the silverware, then organizing the drawers it went in. I found mouse droppings across the counter tops and had to rid all evidence and existence of vermin from my house for good.

"Huh, what?" I answered, surprised.

"Have you been doing this every night? No wonder you're so tired." He took the rag from my hand and began leading me back to bed.

"But, James, the mice are back. There is scat on the counters and I can't let them get into the food stores. Hetty and I will work all night, I can rest tomorrow."

It made no sense. James looked worried at the mention of Hetty because, although I had seen her from time to time, I made no mention of her.

"Hetty is here?"

"Yes, she's starting on that end of the kitchen and I'm starting here. Now give me back my rag so I can work."

"How about you show me where the mice have been and I'll take care of it?"

I pointed to the droppings leading from the doorway, along the edges of the kitchen, parlor, and back hallway. I dropped my rag in place of the broom and started sweeping furiously at the scat.

"Iona, you're tired. Please go to bed."

I knew James wouldn't give up, so I gave Hetty a disapproving glance so she knew how perturbed I was and followed him back to our room. In the morning, the kitchen was spotless. My husband had rid us of the vermin and had the girls fed and dressed for the day.

"Thank you, James. It's very nice to start the day like this."

"Well, I thought perhaps you could use a break. Jennifer was asking about the girls so I thought I'd bring them to her for the morning."

"That would be nice, but it's not necessary. I can take care of them, I am okay."

"Iona, you were cleaning like a mad woman last night, and you kept showing me traces of mice that were not there. Iona, do you hear me? There weren't any mice. Plus, Hetty was with you."

"I know. Hetty has been here a lot. James, I know she isn't real, but I can't help when she shows up. She has good intentions, she really does, she doesn't want me to lose you so she helps me clean and keep order."

"What about the mice? You are so tired you are seeing things. I am worried, honey. I want you to be well. One day you can't get out of bed, the next you spend crying, and then I find you scouring the place at night."

"You knew what you married, James. I never said I was sane, or perfect. I cry and often I feel sad; my body is so heavy it just wants to quit. Then I hear the girls, or you walk through the door and I want to try. I want to do better. Just let me be."

"But that's just it, you are so hard on yourself, dear. You don't have to try so hard. I love you just as you are, for who you are. You are the mother of my children, and I love you. How can I help?"

"Just go to work and don't worry about me." James was reluctant, but he got dressed, packed a lunch, and left.

Hetty tried to offer comfort, but the girls kept interrupting our conversations. I spanked Lucy's bottom when she refused to let me be and she ran off into the parlor sulking. She carried her special baby blanket with her, it was unraveling at the edge and I put it on my list to fix that night.

The baby was sleeping soundly so I went to the coop to collect eggs and have a moment alone. I just needed to sit and breathe in the fresh air. I collected a half dozen brown eggs and lay them carefully in my basket. Then I sat and closed my eyes. I must have nodded off because I woke to the baby's cries. I quickly grabbed the basket and forced my body to walk forward back into my house.

"Suzette, it's all right." I picked up my baby and allowed her to nurse even though it hadn't been a full three hours since her last feeding. She ate frantically on the right side and I alternated her to the left.

"Lucy?" I called out for Lucy, who was never far from her sister. I worried about how long I had slept in the coop and called out for her again.

I stood with the baby and called out as I searched the house. A sinking feeling settled in my gut and I ran outside, I screamed at the top of my lungs, "Lucy! Come here right this minute!"

"If you are playing hide and seek you need to come out. Lucy? You are scaring mommy."

I ran behind the house, toward the garden but I couldn't find Lucy anywhere.

I put my finger against my nipple to break Suzette's suction. I placed her in her crib and although she was crying, I had to find Lucy. After searching the house and surrounding property to no avail for half an hour or more, I knew I had to get my husband.

I ran the two miles to the mill, leaving the baby in her crib so I could get here faster.

"James!" I screamed as I approached. He heard me at once and stopped what he was doing.

"Iona, what is it, are you okay? Where are the girls?" he asked frantically.

"I can't find Lucy! James, I can't find her." I told him I put the baby in her crib after I nursed her and ran all the way here to fetch him. The men at the mill stopped working and formed a search party for my daughter. I went back to Suzette while the men paired off into teams going in all possible directions. James stayed behind to get the rest of the story.

"I scolded Lucy for interrupting me, she sulked into the parlor and played with her blocks. I nursed the baby and put her down to nap, went to the coop for eggs and fell asleep. James, I didn't mean to, I just closed my eyes for a minute."

"Then what happened?" he asked calmly.

"I heard the baby crying and woke up, nursed her again, and called out for Lucy. I thought she was playing hide and seek, James."

"We will find her, Iona. You didn't do anything wrong."

But I knew I did. I had done the unforgivable and let Hetty back in. I scolded my daughter because she was interrupting my discussion with Hetty. Hetty was on my back about the rugs and I just didn't care about their cleanliness. I was telling Hetty to leave me be, but Lucy was being a bother and needing my constant attention. I didn't have the patience for her at the moment so I sent her away with a spank to her bottom and warning to hush. She whimpered softly, as she dragged her blanket behind her toward the parlor. My heart broke because I knew I owed her an apology, and intended to give her one just as soon as we found her.

The men would find her. There were ten of them and she couldn't have gotten too far, but then I thought of the river. Oh, God. Please, God, no. Don't let her have tried to cross the river. She knew how to get to the river's edge because we often walked there for our picnics. She was always tempted to dip her toes in, and we were fearful one day she'd wander down alone and try to swim.

A few men came back but they didn't have Lucy with them. They got drinks and set off in a new direction. Some men brought dogs, and others brought rifles. I sank to the ground with Suzette in my arms and cried.

CHAPTER TWELVE

SORROW

Lucy was found face down in the river. Her lifeless body was swollen and blue when they returned her to me. I was in a state of shock, my hands were cold and my breath was shallow. I had to lie down and close my eyes, close it out and wake from this nightmare. My husband's wails pierced my ears and my heart, he and I were inconsolable. We climbed into bed and held each other, needing to be touched and soothed. Jennifer took the baby for a few days and I let my milk run dry. I sprouted gray hairs overnight and sank into a deep impenetrable depression.

James tried to tell me that Lucy's death was not my fault, but it was. I was solely responsible for her well-being and I neglected her. I hated Hetty for making me fail in such a life-altering way. Hetty cried into her handkerchief over our loss as she stood at my doorway, but I refused to let her in.

"Who are you talking to?" James asked the morning after Lucy was discovered.

"I am telling Hetty to leave now, forever. It's her fault!" I yelled so she would hear. I started banging my fists against the wall and bashing my head against the counters. James grabbed my hands and pulled me in.

"Stop this," he ordered.

I slunk to the ground and wanted to die. My heart was overflowing with grief and pain so deep that I no longer wanted to live. I cried myself to sleep and when I woke, I searched the kitchen for a knife. I found a sharp blade and began sawing at my wrist. Tiny droplets of blood began to drip on the floor and as the pain intensified, I felt woozy. I dropped the instrument and collapsed.

When I woke, I was in bed. My left wrist had linen wrapped around it but blood still soaked through. It needed to be changed. James came in and offered me a sip of water. He unwrapped my hand, but I refused to look at the cut. He cleaned it and put an emollient over the laceration before bandaging it.

"What is wrong with you? Do you think you are the only one who is hurting? You thought you would be selfish and try to take your own life so you don't have to feel anything? What about me?" He began to shake and scream at me.

"Huh, what about me and Suzette? You would just leave us so willingly, like we didn't matter at all?"

I was sapped of all my energy. I had no words and didn't reply. I just closed my eyes and willed myself to die. The next time I woke, James was sleeping in our rocker. He heard the bedsprings and came to my side immediately.

"Iona, please drink something, I need you. I can't live without you." He begged, but I remained still and closed my eyes once more. My husband cried until there were no tears left, and still he whimpered and then dry heaved. I closed him out. I refused to think of my children and pretended they were nothing more than visions. Hetty and Lucy held hands and played a game of patty cake while I watched. I hated Hetty now, but I hated myself more. I was angry with myself for being who I was, a delusional woman who brought children into the world, and for that I needed to be punished.

For everyone around me, time went on. James had to return to work and the baby required care. I didn't budge from bed. I soiled my nightgowns and sheets, and refused to eat, drink, or move. James lifted me and transferred me to the couch when the bed needed changing, and he raised my arms to put me in a fresh gown daily. Every day he put water and crackers at my bedside, and then left.

I didn't know or care who had Suzette, she was better off with anyone but me. I rolled myself into a ball and rocked back and forth, reeling with guilt.

James was full of emotion. I heard him weeping at night, as he lay turned away from me, trying to sleep on his side of the bed. I wanted to reach out to him, but I couldn't. I was dying inside and the only way to hurry the process was to shut everyone out and turn off my humanity.

I heard James in a concentrated discussion with someone in the kitchen, and a short while later, Suzette was brought to me. Tears escaped my eyes at the sight of her. I was afraid I would only hurt her too, so I rolled over and ignored her presence.

"She needs a doctor, James. Right now she merely exists in her room, she is not living and you aren't qualified to heal her."

"Jennifer, she has been traumatized. She will be fine. If you can help with Suzette during the day, I will handle everything at night." James refused to betray my trust and ever run the risk of having me admitted to an insane asylum again.

"But the two of you are so young; you don't have anyone else to help you, James. Let me keep the baby a while longer so that you can try to get her medical attention. How long can you keep this up?"

Weeks led to months, and when I allowed myself to glance at James, he looked like a ghost. He was gaunt and thin, overworked, tired, and suffering. I knew I was deserting him and he couldn't continue this way for much longer. He missed the baby and eventually brought her home at night. He always brought her into the bedroom when she was alert and held her out for me to see, or if my eyes were closed, to hear.

I started looking forward to the evenings. I didn't want to allow myself to feel, but when Suzette was right in front of me, my heart broke with yearning. At night, James sang her lullabies and tucked her into her cradle, which he positioned beside him. He would come to me then, wipe away my tears with his gentle fingers and kiss me on the cheek. Every night he said he loved me and that he wouldn't give up on me. Every night he told me Lucy was in heaven and that it was an accident.

Every night his mercy took hold of my heart and brought me out of my shell a little bit more. It was his kindness alone that allowed me to begin to find the strength to forgive myself, and Hetty. He loved me back to health one moment, one day at a time.

One morning when James left with Suzette for work, I unrolled myself from the balled up fetal position I had adopted. I opened my arms, exposing my chest. I felt the air rush in and fill my lungs and lay my hand across my heart to feel its soft beating.

"God," I whispered, "If you are listening, I need to ask you why? Why was I born this way?" I paused for a moment, thinking of the diagnosis Dr. Macy gave me. I sipped some of the stale water at my bedside before continuing.

"God, are you punishing me for being a defiant child? I would take it all back if I could, but then I wouldn't have gone to Willard and met James. His love for me is more real than anything else in this life. I get confused sometimes, God. I don't always know if a person is real, if they are truly talking to me, or if I am making them up. But when James is beside me, I feel his love and I know, without a doubt that it's real. It penetrates the barriers I built over the years and fills my heart, just as my girls do. What do I do, God? How do I keep living without my precious daughter? Do I let my husband go and build a life with someone better, more deserving of him? How do I live when my daughter is buried in the ground?"

A shuffling sound caused me to open my eyes, standing before me with tears in her eyes was Jennifer. She heard my prayer, and I wondered if God hadn't sent her to me, at precisely this moment for a reason.

"I just wanted to be here, in case you needed anything," Jennifer said in explanation before hugging me tight and crying for both of us.

"Then where is Suzette?" I asked anxiously, suddenly needing to know she was okay.

"She is here, in the parlor, sleeping. She has been napping for three hours mid-morning. I was hoping you'd let me take care of you too?" I nodded yes to her and decided she was the answer to my prayers.

She filled a tub with warm water and stripped me of my soiled nightgown. She took my hand, ever so gently, and led me to the bathroom where she bathed me and washed my hair. She kneaded my scalp and soaped my back. After she rinsed and dried me, she put lotion on my legs, my feet, and hands. She took her time pampering me with the grace of a mother's love. Jennifer was a mother, so she understood my torment and guilt. She brought me into the parlor and sat me down on the davenport while she made tea and checked on the baby.

"Would you like to talk about it?" she asked, placing a steaming mug of tea beside me.

"I didn't deserve Lucy, and I don't deserve James and Suzette."

"You may feel that way now, Iona, but you don't get to choose who loves you. I have seen you with your family and I can say firsthand what an excellent mother you are. You showed Lucy nothing but love in her two years." Jennifer stifled her tears.

"But it is my fault. I scolded for reasons I can't explain. I shouldn't have done that. I thought she was safe in the house when I went to collect the eggs. I needed a minute. I closed my eyes to rest for just a moment…"

"I know, I know. But it was an accident, Iona. You didn't seek to harm your daughter, and we all scold our children for various reasons."

I was at a crossroads. I needed to decide how much I trusted Jennifer. If, in fact, she were a loyal friend, then she would be able to listen to my story and understand the real reason I felt at fault. If I doubted that she was real, or that our friendship was honorable, then I needed to keep my secret locked away. Her eyes sought mine for understanding.

"I am tired, Jennifer. But I do want you to understand that there is more to the story. I'd like to tell you if you'd be willing to listen."

"I am here, aren't I?" The baby stirred for a moment and I turned my ear toward her, but she settled herself once more.

"I had a difficult upbringing. I felt very alone in my home although I did have two siblings, brothers. No one in the family ever really loved me. I suppose they were more concerned with outward appearances. I was continually in trouble for not being more feminine or taking more of an interest in domestic matters. Truthfully, I was just a child, a child who wanted to run free and play outside all day long. I was subject to emotional abuse from a young age. My mother gave me the silent treatment, withheld food from me, and locked me in my room if I failed to do my chores properly or if I sassed her in any way. My father despised me. During this time, I developed an imaginary friend. Her name is Hetty. I wish I could tell you that Hetty went away as I grew up, but in fact, she became a stronger influence. I convinced myself that Hetty was our new housekeeper. She came several days a week and part of her duties included teaching me how to keep house. I scrubbed the tubs with her and learned how to wash floors, laundry became second nature. From there we moved on to the kitchen where she was teaching me some basic cooking techniques. Hetty was as real to me then as you are to me now."

"Okay," Jennifer said, squeezing my hand and encouraging me to continue my story.

"Hetty was more than a figment of my imagination; the doctors said she was a delusion. They said I contrived her to keep me out of trouble, although the revelation she existed is what got me in trouble. But that part comes later. Hetty kept me company when I was locked in my room, forced to repent for being disobedient. She encouraged me to work hard at everything I did. She was larger than life, she was always smiling and singing too, and boy, could she dance." I took a moment to drink my tea and collect myself.

"Until I met you, Hetty was my only friend. That's why I am afraid to share the rest with you, Jennifer. I don't want you to think less of me."

"You can trust me, Iona, we are friends."

"I was sent away because of my disobedience. I cut my hair, was unable to make friends at school, and incidentally, had an imaginary friend, Hetty. My parents had me admitted to the Willard Hospital for the Insane. I doubt they had any intention of me returning home, this was evident by their lack of correspondence. I met James at Willard. James, mind you, was there from the time he was a small boy through no fault of his own. It is his story to tell, but trust me when I say that he never belonged there and that he is not insane or troubled in any way. He tended the animals at the farm and I worked in the stables, which is how we met and fell in love. I was being tortured daily.

I won't go into the details, but I fell gravely ill and nearly died. As soon as I was healthy enough, I escaped. James and I planned to marry one day. We talked about settling in Waterloo, so when I ran he came here straight away to find me. It was a chance he took, but he found me. We were married that night and have made it on our own for three years now. We owe a lot to Ben for giving him a job and to you for helping with my home." I gestured to the walls around me, so much that I learned came from this woman.

"You have been more than a friend, Jennifer. You are like a mother to me and a grandmother to my girls. Lucy was lucky to have had you in her life."

"Well, that is quite a story."

"I have to finish. After Suzette was born, I felt very melancholy. I was not myself; you suggested it was the baby blues. I was tired and overwhelmed all day, and then felt guilty for not working harder on the house. Hetty forced me up at night to do chores. We scoured the place then, until James caught me and forced me back to bed. The house started to fall apart, I was tired, Suzette wanted to nurse all the time, and sweet Lucy just wanted my attention. I was arguing with Hetty about the rugs, of all things, when Lucy kept interrupting. I told her to go away and swatted her bottom. She took her blanky into the parlor and lay down. I never went to her. I knew she was safe, and the baby was sleeping so I took a moment for myself. It was selfish and I would give anything to have the moment back. I loved that darling angel more than life."

Jennifer held me for a long time. "She was so lucky to have your love. Do you know how much your love meant to her? You hugged her one hundred times a day, sang to her, played with her and made sure she had everything she needed. It's okay to need a break. How many hugs did your mother give you?"

"Not many."

"I suspected that."

"Well, I blame Hetty."

We both laughed at how preposterous that sounded. Then a remarkable thing occurred.

"Hetty, join us." Jennifer beckoned for Hetty to come out from the kitchen and sit with us.

I moved over to make room for her wide girth, and then that girl sat down between us as if she truly belonged. Just then, the baby stirred, and although I had yet to regain my strength, I stood to go get her. She was waiting, smiling at her mother, the woman who loved her more than life itself.

From that moment forward, I knew that as sure as I was alive, Hetty was part of me. Those people in my life, who truly loved me to the depths of my soul, understood this.

Together, my faithful husband, my angelic daughter, and my true friend loved me back to a health.

CHAPTER THIRTEEN

TOPHER

When Suzette was six years old, she developed an imaginary friend. She named her friend Topher and spent hours clomping through the outdoors with him by her side. Often they would play chase, or pick dandelions and make wishes. Sometimes they played dolls, which Topher didn't like, or marbles, which he did.

In early September, I peered out the window and watched my daughter raking the leaves that had fallen from our maples into one large pile. She laughed and jumped into the mountain, flattening it as her bottom hit the heap only to gather and fluff the leaves once more so that Topher could have a turn. Suzette never left Topher out, and even became insistent that he have a place at our table for mealtimes.

I wondered if my daughter, who played so innocently, was vulnerable to seeing things as I was. It concerned her father and me immensely. We decide to oblige her whim for the meantime and address it if it became a serious issue down the road.

"Tophy is hungry, Mama. He needs supper too." She said, looking up at me with wide eyes. I would pretend to plate whatever we had to eat for Topher and put it in front of his imaginary chair but this did not suffice.

"No, Mama, Topher needs real food and his own chair. Baby John can move over to make room."

So I moved the highchair with Johnathan in it closer to me and put a plate of real food in front of the chair with Topher who eagerly waited for supper. When Suzette's milk spilled all over the table and dripped down the sides, she exclaimed, "Topher is sorry, he had an accident."

I wiped the mess and said directly to Topher's chair, "Topher, please be more careful with your milk."

Suzette smiled when I talked directly to Topher and carried on as usual.

"Should we be worried?" James asked me after the milk incident that night. We had tucked the children into bed giving us a chance to speak alone.

"I know you don't want her to be persecuted when she starts school next week. I am worried too, but if anything is going to help her, it's getting her acquainted with other children her age so that she can start making some real friends. I love our home, but it is secluded, James, she only has me all daylong and half the time I am tending the baby. I honestly think this is the right choice."

"When did you start to see Hetty?"

"I was much older, fourteen, I believe. Remember, Dr. Macy told me years and years ago that many children have imaginary friends and that it can be a normal part of growing up."

"Yes, but how will we know if it's more than just an imaginary friend? What if she is stuck with Topher for good? Sorry, Hetty, wherever you are." He glanced around the room apologetically.

"I have come to accept Hetty as part of my life, and thankfully you have too. But, I also understand now that she isn't real to anyone but me. She is a delusion, but this awareness came with age and experience, now I can carry on in public and no one would be the wiser that my friend was beside me. Remember, Hetty helped me through some tough times."

"I know, but she put you through some tougher times."

"Well, I don't think we need to be worried. I think we give it a little time and see what happens in the next few months."

The week went by in a tizzy and soon it was time for Suzette's first day of school.

"How about the purple dress for your first day?" I asked, holding it out to her.

"Topher says no," she replied. Topher was exhausting.

"How about the yellow one then?" I asked, putting the purple one back in place of the sunny yellow dress.

"Topher says yes."

"Okay then, let's get you ready. Hold up your arms for me." I slipped the dress over her underclothes and then we braided her hair and tied pretty bows with green ribbons at the ends.

"You will make so many friends today, I can't wait to hear all about it!"

"Topher is sad."

"Why?"

"He knows he has to stay home and he is going to be lonely."

"Topher can help me with Johnathan, how about that? I'll be sure to keep him busy, okay?"

"Okay. Thank you, Mama."

I felt all the air I had been holding in expel from my chest. Thankfully, Suzette had the wherewithal to realize Topher was better off at home than with her as she started kindergarten. I walked her to school, and lingered as she left me. She was growing up so fast. She didn't cry like some of the other children did, instead she waved me off and ran along confidently.

It was an unseasonably warm day so I pushed Johnathan in his pram toward the mill to share the news with James. As we approached, I could see James from a far as he directed men with sacks of grain toward the warehouse. I admired him as he worked; clearly, the other men respected and looked up to him for his tireless work ethic.

"Darling, what are you two doing here?" He ran toward me, worried something was wrong.

"We thought we'd take a little walk through town today while Suzette was at school. I wanted you to know that Topher is not with her." He took my meaning immediately and hugged me tight.

We had both wanted a normal life for our daughter and felt relieved. After spending a few moments with James, we walked farther into town toward the bakery. I selected a white cake with vanilla icing for tonight's dessert. If there was one thing I did not do, it was deprive my children of dessert as my mother did me. Usually we had berries with cream, or tarts, and pies, but tonight we were having cake.

I carried the cake box atop the pram and took the baby to watch the ducks glide across the pond in town. I found another woman and her small child and we chatted briefly. It turned out her daughter was also starting kindergarten today. We decided perhaps sometime in the next week we would allow the girls to play together after school.

Soon it was time to gather Suzette from school, I waited outside her building and my heart soared when I saw her holding the hands of two other girls. I knew she was capable of making friends and this proved it.

"Mama," she yelled and ran toward me for a hug.

"How was your first day?" I asked, but could tell from the huge smile she wore that she enjoyed herself immensely.

"I made friends, Mama, and the teacher taught us how to write our letters. Can I show you?"

"Of course, let's get home and you can show me everything."

That night we had cake and felt the sweet blessings of the day.

CHAPTER FOURTEEN

CAT

The following morning after the same rigmarole of selecting an outfit that met Topher's approval, we dressed, ate breakfast, and went to school. I decided to spend the morning at home doing chores, so the baby and I came immediately back to the house.

When I approached our homestead, I noted that the door was ajar. I was certain I had closed it. I had no doubt, for I was always concerned about the barn cats getting inside. The barn cats weren't trustworthy with the baby, one even tried to smother him once, so they were not allowed entrance under any circumstances.

I felt a shiver go up my spine and then I heard the familiar voice. "Hello, Iona."

It was Cat. She looked twenty years older; she was filthy and missing several of her teeth. I didn't want to hug her for her attire smelled something awful. She had a peculiar look in her eye and I suddenly felt very afraid.

Cat held a knife in her hand, but laughed when she saw my eyes glance at it.

"Aren't you happy to see me?" she muttered, somewhat jumpy.

"Cat. Why, of course I am, it's just unexpected. Please, sit, let me make us some tea."

"Got any food? I am starving."

"How about I make you some eggs?" I wondered why she was here and who else she had brought to my door. I cracked four eggs and scrambled them with water, put a dollop of butter in the frying pan and let them set while I made toast. Cat inhaled her food and I offered to make her more. She was afraid if she ate more she would vomit.

"Cat, where have you been? What happened to you?" I asked gently, putting my hand on top of hers.

"Oh, I've been around," she said evasively, as she made a circle in the air with her fork.

"Did you find Samuel?" I had to know if she found her husband.

"Oh, I found him alright, he already forgot about me though. He was bedding another young girl when I made it to him. I was sick, you remember, and he wouldn't even take me in. He threatened to return me to my father's home if I didn't leave. So, I pretended to leave, waited for night to fall, stole the money I knew he kept hidden in his church shoes and ran."

"I went to Rochester and spent time in a little town called Penfield. It was nice, but got boring after a while. I've been traveling a bit here and there. Thought I'd come see how you were making out."

"Well, James and I are married. We have two children now and things have worked themselves out."

"That's good, that's good," Cat said. She was fidgety and kept glancing outside, which caused me to wonder about her state of mind.

"How about if we get you cleaned up? I could draw you a bath and you can stay with us tonight if you need a place."

"Okay, yes, yes." She was repeating herself and looking around nervously. She grabbed for the baby, but I swooped him into my arms before she could get a hold of him.

"Here is the bathroom. Hand me out your clothes and I'll

give you something of mine to wear." Cat was about five feet and six inches tall, but she was so thin now I wouldn't guess she weighed one hundred pounds. She closed the door as she undressed and filled the tub. I thought her wrists looked chafed, but would have to earn her trust before I could get a better look.

It had been nearly eight years since I had laid eyes on the woman who saved my life when we escaped from Willard. So much had happened for me during that time, and the sudden appearance from someone in my past unsettled me.

I clomped off the mud on her shoes and started washing her clothing. Honestly, I wanted to burn the garment because I was afraid it was infested with lice or worse. When an hour past, I knocked gently on the bathroom door, "Cat, it's me, can I come in?" When Cat didn't answer, I opened the door. Across her chest was the raised flesh of an angry scar that was ten or eleven inches long. Her wrists had fresh wounds that needed treatment, the cuts were deep and infected, causing me to think she was recently shackled. Why? What could have happened to this woman?

"Cat, I need to clean your wounds." The timbre of my voice relayed the seriousness of the situation. I brought iodine and cotton balls into the bathroom, and prayed the baby wouldn't fuss. I laid the medicine across a towel gently dabbed at her wrists with warm water. The tub water was murky, so I pulled the drain to empty the filth. She lay naked, unabashed in the empty tub and closed her eyes as it refilled.

I left her to soak and went into our bedroom where we kept our worldly goods. I retrieved our money from my dresser drawer and stuffed the roll of bills into my bodice, I only owned two pieces of jewelry so I stuffed them in my bodice as well. I needed to pick up Suzette in a few hours and felt paranoid about leaving Cat alone in my home. I had no doubt she would paw through our belongings and take whatever she liked in payment for setting me free years ago. I had no doubt Cat had an agenda, I just needed to figure it out. I told her I needed to go to school, but that I'd return within in the hour.

I ran to school with Johnathan and thankfully, I wasn't late retrieving Suzette. I spoke briefly with the teacher who adored her and we left. On the way home, I took a detour to Jennifer's home with the children.

"Grandma Jenny wants to hear all about school so I promised her a visit."

"Yippee, I hope Grammy made us oatmeal raisin cookies!" My daughter chimed as she skipped ahead of me.

We knocked on the door of Jennifer's home and I thanked my lucky stars when she answered. She immediately recognized the anguish on my face and I pulled her aside while Suzette busied herself in the play area Jennifer set up for the kids.

"Can you watch the kids tonight?"

"Of course, what on earth is wrong?"

"Cat, I told you about her, she is at the house and she isn't right…"

"Does James know?"

"No, and I don't want her to get suspicious if I am gone too long, so I can't run to the mill and tell him."

"I will. Now you be careful, not everyone who escaped Willard was meant to. Maybe you should take the gun?"

"Heavens no, I couldn't. I am sure everything will be fine, I just need to find out what her game is."

"Be careful, Iona." She hugged me and I said chirpy goodbyes to the children.

When I got home, Cat had seemingly disappeared.

"Cat, where are you? I'm back, let's catch up, where are you?"

She stumbled out from behind the porch door and it was easy to see she had found our whiskey. She held the bottle in one hand and a gleaming knife in the other.

"Remember when I saved your life all those years ago?" She slurred.

"Of course I do, I owe you my freedom. What do you need, Cat, tell me so that I can help."

She put the knife down and sat with the bottle of whiskey. Taking a long gulp, she hiccupped and launched into her story.

"I have to get away from here, they'll be after me in no time."

"Who, Cat, who will be after you?"

"Same mean bastard who gave me this scar."

"Cat, did you lead them here?" She ignored the question.

"See I had a ruse going, and it worked pretty well for a time. I dressed up real nice and pretty and pretended to be interested in buying a horse and carriage that I found listed for sale in the paper. I showed up to the address acting all ladylike with a purse full of money so the sellers knew I was capable of managing the purchase. I'd ask to take the animals out for a jaunt to see how they behaved. Usually the folks was unsuspecting and let me take the horses with the carriage too, and then I never returned."

"You're a horse thief?" I wanted her out of my house at once.

"That I am. I'd sell the animals the next town over and for a few years, I made a living this way. Until eventually, someone recognized their horse and people started to put two and two together. One mean son of a bitch tracked me down. Truth was, he was thieving horses too, and he's the one that sliced me open so I'd stay out of his way. Left me for dead too, but his brother, William, took pity on me. He was slow in the head, didn't talk much, but tried to patch me up. I made nice with him and grew to like his odd ways. His brother saw how happy I made him and after much debate, the group decided I could help by posing as a rich widow needing to buy horses, only difference now was they got to keep the money. A small price for my life.

"Gracious. We can't let them find you, Cat. You'll be hung for sure."

"Ain't you gonna ask me how I escaped?"

"Sure, I suppose, but right now I'm more concerned how to keep you hidden."

Then a booming voice behind me said, "Too late for that, ladies."

A man with a pistol had entered my home, he had two or three men outside, and they all had guns and rifles too. He looked me up and down in a way that made me feel dirty and then his eyes settled on Cat.

"So we meet again," he said gravely.

"Sir, please, I'll pay whatever she owes," I interrupted him as he approached Cat.

"She only told you half the story, I'm afraid. It's true, we got in a little scuffle when she got in the way of my con, costing me time and money. I might have been able to get over that, but then she got in tight with my brother and convinced us she was gonna join our little gang, that she was working for us now. We could hear her and my brother going at it all night long too. She's a feisty one, we thought she was good for him because he was dim-witted and ain't never had a woman before. Then my brother caught her stealing his roll and attempting to run. That's when she shackled him and burned down the barn we was hiding in. She damn near burned him alive and we would have all died too but we left the building to sleep under the stars so we didn't have to hear 'em grunting no more. One of the men heard them fighting and ran to see what was going on, he made it out of the flames alive and told us everything. My brother died the next day from his wounds. We tracked her and once we found her, we tied her up good, but somehow this one always gets away. Should have shot her then. Ain't making that mistake twice. I am here to see justice is done." The man spit a wad of chewing tobacco right on my floor without a single care.

I looked from the man with the pistol to the men outside. They were an unruly bunch that one did not tangle with. I reached into my blouse and pulled out the wad of bills, I handed them forward and begged them to leave. The front man released his trigger and aimed the barrel of his gun right at Cat. She never flinched, she stared him down, willing him to kill a woman.

"You gonna kill the woman that's carrying your brother's child?" she taunted.

He was caught off guard by her words, but pointed the gun anyway, and that's when we heard the sounds of rifles going off outside.

Jennifer had made a run to town with the children in tow. She told James that I looked like I had seen a ghost. James, Don, the sheriff, and several other men surrounded the place now. One of the ruffians started shooting wildly into the house, so Cat and I sunk down to the ground. The man inside grabbed my hair and lifted Cat up and over his shoulder, then he walked right outside with us as his hostages.

"Hear me!" he yelled. "I got a fine woman here, you put your guns down and let my men go or she will be coming with me."

"Leave both the women unharmed," the sheriff yelled.

"No, sir, this one owes me a life; she'll be coming with me."

Just then, James pointed his loaded rifle to the man's back. The man dropped Cat and me and stepped off the porch with his hands up.

"Now drop your weapons, men, we have the house surrounded."

With a rifle pointed at their front man, the men dropped their weapons in unison. The sheriff and his deputy came forward and shackled the men. Then he came for Cat.

"But sheriff, she's pregnant!"

"She doesn't look pregnant to me."

Cat lifted her dress and, sure enough, she had a round, firm, baby bump I had not noticed before. I suppose I didn't notice because I was focused on her scar and the fresh wounds on her wrists. She didn't look more than three months along, but now I understood why she thought she would vomit her meal of eggs.

CHAPTER FIFTEEN

WILLARD ONCE MORE

"Sir, you cannot keep a pregnant woman in jail," I argued with the sheriff.

"With all due respect, this pregnant woman is a criminal. We are holding her for murder, arson, and the theft of over a dozen horses. I can't let her go. However, if you can think of an alternative, I would consider it, but otherwise she will stay here until her trial."

"Can I see her?" I asked, concerned about her health.

"I don't see the harm. Come on, follow me." The sheriff led me down a narrow hallway to the dank jail cell they concocted specially for Cat. They had a few drunks sleeping off the night's charades in the front cells and seeing as she was pregnant, were allowing her some privacy.

I hugged Cat from across a table, "Why didn't you tell me you were pregnant? Why didn't you come to me before?"

"It wouldn't have mattered," she said with trembling voice.

"I could have helped, but now you'll be charged with murder, and arson, and theft. You'll be hung, Cat. Unless…"

"Unless what?"

"Unless this baby matters to you."

"It does." She put a protective hand over her bump and smiled ever so slightly.

"There is one solution. You could go back to Willard Hospital. They accepted pregnant patients years ago and I am sure they will now. You can have the baby there, and I will visit you as often as I can. I will care for and love your baby is if it were my own."

"As soon as the baby is born they would hang me, so either way it doesn't matter."

"It matters because you'd be kept alive at Willard if you are declared insane. That means you can remain in touch with the baby. I can send you photographs, and letters with updates. Jennifer could pose as the child's grandmother and bring him to visit."

"This presumes you'd be willing to take a chance on my child? What if he or she is dumb like its father?" Cat asked.

"We will love the child regardless. We have a happy home, Cat, the baby would have siblings to grow up with." I looked into her empty, sad eyes that, up until now, had been full of torment and regret. Now I thought I saw a flicker of hope.

"How did it all go so wrong for me, Iona? Does this baby even stand a chance?" She was vulnerable and I could see it in her eyes.

"I want you to think about this, I'll come back tomorrow and we can talk some more." I had to think about this as well. It wasn't the baby's fault that he or she would be born into such dire circumstances. It deserved a good life and I could give it that. Still, I needed to discuss it with James.

Cat had become careless in her appearance and drank alcohol freely, she had difficulty sleeping and couldn't secure an honest job. She committed crimes, yet did this qualify her to be subject once more to Willard? Just reminiscing about my short stint there made me emotional. Memories of shuffling, catatonic patients took over my mind and I knew at once I didn't want to see Cat like that. We would hire a lawyer for her, the best in town, and plead not guilty to the charge of murder. I would personally take on work to pay back all the money she earned from stealing horses. She was shifty, it was true, and I didn't trust her entirely. Yet she stuck her neck out for me once and it made all the difference. She needed tender care, she needed three solid meals a day, a warm bath, and to know she was loved.

She hadn't known true love a day in her life. It was no wonder why then as a young girl she was loud and boisterous. She wanted someone to notice her. Isn't that what we all want, to matter to someone in this world? To be seen and heard? I paid extra attention to my family when I returned home. Touching everyone and hugging them so they knew they were dear to me. When James and I settled in for the night, I rubbed his back and kissed him fully and deeply as he liked.

"Thank you, James. You saved my life."

"That scoundrel never would have gotten away with you, all the men in town were coming to help."

"That's because they all respect you. I am grateful you snuck up on him, but I meant thank you for loving me. Without you and the children, I would feel empty and I owe my happiness to you. Cat has never known what that feels like. I should have asked you first, but I told her we would take the baby."

"I figured you would say that," he said, tucking a tendril of my hair behind my ear.

"Are you mad?"

"No. That child deserves a chance at a normal and happy upbringing from the beginning. I can't help but think Cat knew this would go down just like it did. I think she wanted you to take the baby, think about it. She could have run toward Freeville or Canandaigua, but she ran to you. She knew they would follow and she'd be put in jail too. She thought it through, Iona, and as angry as I am at her for getting you involved and putting you in harm's way, she was right to come here."

"I told her there was a way she could live. Now, even I see the idea was haphazard. I suggested she admit herself to Willard once more. I was thinking she could give birth and then stay on as a lifer. She would be placed in a strict ward I have no doubt, but my thought was she could receive updates about the baby. Maybe even see him one day for a visit."

"It's not a bad idea, but I just can't fathom she would willingly go back to that place. If Patty were still there, she'd be in trouble from day one. I suppose the alternative, though, is worse. If she had the baby in jail and handed him to us, she'd be led to trial and found guilty, then hung. I guess it comes down to how much more she is willing to take.

"And how much she loves her baby," I said with mixed emotions.

CHAPTER SIXTEEN

DANIEL

"Cat, I came as soon as I got word." I heard Cat was in labor and ran to the jail to help her bring the child she carried into the world. The sheriff agreed to keep her prisoner until she gave birth as a personal favor to us. It would have been easier to send her off to Willard, but this way I could see her daily and nurse her back to health during the pregnancy.

I found my friend, if you could call her that, in the throes of labor. She was squatting and rubbing her lower back with one hand while the other was firmly on the ground to stabilize her. I didn't have back labor with any of my children, but Jennifer had and said it was dreadful.

"Get this thing out of me!" Cat screamed, at her wit's end.

"Okay, lay back on the cot and let me have a look."

I lifted Cat's skirt and indeed, she was fully dilated. I ordered her to push when she felt the need and as she did, she began to tear ever so slightly. With each successive push, the baby's head crowned until finally I could see his eyes, his nose, mouth, and then shoulders. I cradled his shoulders and pulled him into the world.

"It's a boy, Cat."

"I don't care," she said, turning her head away from the newborn. She was sick and tired from nearly seven long months in jail and felt it was best not to create ties with the child who would be taken from her anyway.

"He is crying for you, he needs your comfort," I said, handing her the swaddled baby boy.

"He is going to be ripped from me in a day or two, so what good will my comfort do him?"

"Here, just hold him. Look at him, Cat, this is your son."

She turned her head shyly toward the baby and awkwardly held out her arms to receive the bundle. She cradled the baby for a moment, weeping all the while. After five minutes of studying his features, Cat pushed him back into my arms. She then curled herself into a ball on the cot, facing the cinder blocks.

"What do you want to name him?" I asked gently.

"He is your child, Iona, you name him."

"Oh, no. Surely, you must name him. He needs a strong name to carry through all his days."

After much deliberation, Cat settled on the name Daniel James for her son. The adoption took place the following afternoon. Cat signed the child over to James and me and we took him into the folds of our family, making Jennifer and her husband the godparents.

Cat had one day left with her child before going back to Willard. She didn't want to die or rot in a jail cell for the remainder of her days. Instead, she agreed that by living out her days at Willard she would at least have the chance to receive news of Daniel's growth and progress. She could receive photographs and letters too. She decided she didn't want the child to know her, she would take a back seat to his upbringing, instilling her trust fully in me.

PART
TWO

.

CHAPTER SEVENTEEN

PRESENT DAY

My grandmother, Iona, was mentally ill. The rumor in the family was that she had spent several years in an insane asylum before stealing a horse and escaping. Not that it was okay to steal a horse, but if she hadn't done that, I wouldn't be here. Nor would my family or my granddaughter, Jenna.

Afraid the disease was hereditary, I watched both of my children for signs of anything unusual as they grew up. Lucky for me, and them, they are both "normal" according to society's definition.

However, my granddaughter, Jenna, is another story. I have deep concerns about her and worry about her future.

When Jenna was born, the family was delighted. Jenna was the first girl cousin among a gaggle of boys. She was born to my daughter, Camille, and was her only child. As she grew from a toddler to adolescent, her tendencies toward the dramatic were attributed to her gender and the fact she had been doted on since birth. Everyone clamored to hold her when she was little and bestowed all kinds of lavish gifts upon her…just because. Jenna was in the spotlight and she expected to be the center of attention.

Jenna's only stumbling block as a small child was her speech and language delay along with her short attention span. A speech pathologist worked with Jenna once a week over the course of a year and eventually she caught up to her peers. Jenna's pediatrician suggested that she might have had a mild case of

Attention Deficit Disorder. This would account for the difficulty she had in a classroom setting paying attention to the teacher.

She had a few neighborhood friends and when they got together, they created short plays and musicals. They would raid their parents' closets for costumes and set designs, and spend hours drafting elaborate, sparkly invitations and drawing posters. The kids would practice their show for weeks before the big day until it was perfect. Then my daughter Camille's garage was transformed from a dark cavernous place used to store junk into a theater in the round. The audience members paid one dollar per person to attend and in return were offered paper cups of hot buttered popcorn when they took their seats. Jenna was often the star of the show, draped in boas, wearing heels and make-up, not shy or fearful of having eyes on her in the least. So when she turned twelve and began to shy away from creating plays and other social activities that she used to love, I became concerned.

Besides her social withdrawal, other behaviors became more pronounced, behaviors that I thought were cause for alarm. Jenna began wearing rubber boots in the shower to protect herself, but from what she couldn't identify. She was more often forgetful, losing everything from her sweaters and coats, to her school books. She talked to herself incessantly, but in a language neither her mother nor I could understand. Most troubling and off-putting, however, was the licking and smelling of objects. This didn't just occur in the privacy of our home, but also when we went out in public. My granddaughter was oblivious to the odd looks she received when she licked a wall, or sniffed the contents of a garbage can. She seemed to me as if she were in her own world at times. She would lick her palms several times an hour, drag them along the walls, and then raise them to her nostrils and inhale deeply to smell them. She smelled her feet, her armpits, and her hair. Chewing on her hair was not upsetting, because so many young girls did this, but Jenna could not stop. To my dismay, she would kneel on all fours and lap the cement front porch where we sat having lemonade on a sunny afternoon, or the driveway, or kitchen floor. It wasn't until she lapped the toilet seat in the grocery store that I admitted something was dreadfully wrong.

I accompanied Jenna into the bathroom at *Wegman's* where I could see her through the crack. I had asked her to line the toilet seat before she sat to pee, but instead she knelt down and licked it. I gagged and held in the bile that formed at the back of my throat. Rather than shop, when my granddaughter came out from the stall, I took her home and called her mother immediately. Jenna needed an intervention. My daughter rushed home from work because I told her there was an emergency. She thought Jenna had broken a bone, was extremely ill, or worse. When I relayed the facts of my morning with her, my daughter was not surprised.

"She does that all the time, well not the toilet seat, but the licking."

"She could get seriously ill. Honey, something needs to be done. It's not normal," I said, standing my ground.

"I don't know what to do, Mom. She does well in school, and seems to be happy. It's just a phase."

"Do you really think so, Camille? I see a child who is lonely and sick." More and more Jenna's behaviors reminded me of my grandmother, Iona, and I couldn't bite my tongue any longer. I was concerned given my family history and expressed this to my daughter, but she was dismissive.

"Mom, she is not lonely or sad, look how happy she is." Camille was in denial.

We both looked at Jenna who was humming a familiar radio tune and staring into space. She did appear content, but I wouldn't consider her happy. She didn't invite friends over anymore, was often irritable, and had become increasingly difficult to please. The harder she was to gratify, the harder everyone around her tried to appease her and the more her mother ignored her odd behaviors. But I couldn't ignore what I saw today.

"I think you need to take her to a doctor, Camille. Something is wrong."

"Mom, back off. Nothing is wrong with my daughter. I would appreciate it if you'd stay with her the rest of the afternoon, I need to get back to work."

Today was a staff development day at Jenna's school, which is why I was spending the morning with her. My apartment was only a few miles down the road and I was retired so I didn't mind.

"Okay, fine. Have a good day," I said to Camille as she left.

I watched my granddaughter scowl, then lick her hands, this time the palms and the tops, concentrating on her knuckles. Then she smelled her feet, spreading her toes one at a time and picked at the skin in between them. She stood up and twirled around three times before flopping onto the couch and claiming she was bored.

"How about if we go to the mall, dear? We could buy you a pretty new outfit, or maybe see a movie?"

"Yes, yes, I want to go shopping!" she exclaimed, as she jumped off the couch and clapped her hands like a little girl.

"Okay, what are we waiting for? Let's go." I grabbed my car keys and we left.

When we got to the mall, Jenna licked the glass panes on the doors to the entrance. Strangers glanced at her oddly as if she were demented. She was not concerned with strangers, and continued to skip along ahead of me toward the center fountain at the mall.

"Grandma, can I have a penny to make a wish?"

I fished through my purse and pulled out two pennies, one for Jenna and one for me. Jenna put the penny in her mouth and swished it between her teeth, sucking on the copper. Then she pulled it out, sniffed it and threw it into the water.

"Why do you do that?" I asked her.

"Leave me alone, Grandma," she spewed rudely and abruptly before stomping away from me. Normally when we went shopping Jenna was a delight, but if this was an indicator for her mood, it was going to be a long day.

I decided to ignore the antics and just press on. I followed Jenna into several stores where she tried on dresses, stretch pants, jeans paired with half tops, and more. Finally, she settled on a mini skirt with flower print and solid colored half top exposing her belly button, as was the fashion these days.

I suggested we eat lunch at *Uno's* and she complied. "So are you happy with your new outfit?" I asked over our pizzas.

"I said, leave me alone, Grandma."

"I'm sorry? Did you say to leave you alone? I just asked if you were happy with your new outfit. Goodness me."

"You always bother me, just don't talk."

Jenna had never, in all her life, treated me so rudely. It had been several months since we had a special day together, but this wasn't her normal behavior at all. It was almost like there were two Jennas. The happy, twirly, jovial Jenna who licked everything, and this mean and nasty Jenna who was, simply put, rude and inappropriate.

I remained quiet for the rest of the meal. I observed Jenna as she sucked the sauce from her mushrooms on her pizza and then put them in a pile on her plate. She ate the pizza, licked the plate, sniffed her hands, and gazed into the distance with a half-smile on her face, seeming oblivious to my hurt feelings.

I paid the restaurant bill, grabbed the leftover bag and drove us straight home. Jenna pulled out the outfit we purchased and threw it to the floor, "Grandma, why would you buy me such a hideous outfit? It's for a little girl, with the flowers, yuck, I hate it." Then she began talking in her special language. She clicked her tongue and spoke so quickly it was near impossible to make out any meaning.

"Give it to me then." I shook my head at her nonsense and I took the outfit, replacing it in the bag along with the receipt. Then I began jotting notes on the pad I kept in my purse. My daughter worked so much that she had no idea what was becoming of her only child or if she did, she wasn't making any plans to rectify it. Divorced for three years now, she bore the burden of raising Jenna. Her ex-husband was not dependable and was only in and out of Jenna's life sporadically. Camille worked two jobs to make ends meet and relied on me to help when she wasn't available.

I often went to Jenna's school open houses, to her chorale concerts and teacher conferences, so I felt I had a say in her upbringing. Next week was the spring concert at school and I was beginning to dread it. I feared Jenna would act out and embarrass us all, but Camille didn't fret one bit. When the day arrived, Jenna came downstairs dressed in black from head to toe and wearing black eye make-up and red lipstick. She was only twelve years old and was far too young for make-up.

"Oh, Jenna, go take that off right now," I said, knowing the kids were supposed to dress in spring attire.

"Mom, she is just experimenting. Gosh," my daughter said in front of Jenna, undermining me.

"So, you are okay with her looking like that?" I asked my daughter.

"Well, no, but what can I do?" she asked me in front of Jenna as if she had no authority over her child, giving Jenna all the power.

I was fearful of going to the concert and bearing witness to Jenna's strange behaviors. I didn't want to be embarrassed but I felt I needed to be present for my daughter.

When the seventh grade took the stage, Jenna was front and center. Her smaller size, when compared to her peers, landed her in the front row. Her black attire stood out among the bright pinks, purples, and blues the other students wore to celebrate the season. When the group sang, Jenna looked far off in the distance, her mouth unmoving. I followed her eyes and noted she was staring at the clock, perhaps she just felt uncomfortable on stage and found the overhead lights to daunting.

Thankfully, when the fourth and final song was complete, the seventh graders were led off stage. No outbursts or odd behaviors took place and I was grateful. When we arrived home, Jenna seemed a tad confused, and sullen. We watched television for an hour or so and before bedtime, Jenna looked utterly confused.

"When is my concert, Grandma?" she asked, in front of her mother.

"Darling, your spring concert was tonight." We were alarmed she forgot the past several hours and knew she was not okay.

"What? Why didn't you take me? I am so mad at you. I hate you! You forced me into this horrible black outfit and why do I have eyeliner on?" Again, Jenna spewed made up words that were confusing and strange.

I looked at my daughter as tears streamed down her face. It wasn't just the licking and smelling anymore, or the short temper, now it was as if Jenna were divided.

CHAPTER EIGHTEEN

GENETICS

My grandmother, Iona, was mentally insane. She spent time in an insane asylum as a young woman for being demented and having delusions. I had fond memories of Iona, however, because she was always a pleasure to be around. Iona was simply an odd duck with imaginary friends that she conversed with. As a child, I used to laugh out loud when my grandmother had a running dialog going with an invisible person, until my mother told me it wasn't kind to make fun.

"But, Mama, no one is there. It's so funny," I would retort.

"It might seem that no one is there to you, Shirley, but to Grandma, her friends are very real," my mother said.

This was my first experience with mental illness and as a result, it made me more observant of the people around me and how they interacted with others.

I saw Grandma Iona in Jenna at times, that distant, confused look that Jenna got worried me and took me back to my youth. Sometimes my grandmother would look lost and afraid, and her condition worsened as she aged, especially after my grandfather, James, died.

Jenna was only twelve years old, true, she didn't seem to have any aberrations or people she spoke to, but her other behaviors pointed to something disturbing.

Camille made the appointment with her pediatrician, who, after observing Jenna, phoned the psychiatric center at Syracuse's premier Hutchings facility. It was a facility that took care of children as well as adults. It had beds for those that needed round the clock care, or offered day treatment options for those less dire.

Our first appointment was with Dr. Saul who would be giving Jenna her psychiatric evaluation. He was very curious upon observing Jenna's behaviors. She licked the walls in his office, sniffed the air like a pup, and then licked her hands. When she sat before him, she took off her shoes and socks, then licked her feet. She had no sense that this was odd or inappropriate. It was as if her sense of right and wrong, along with appropriate manners, were lost.

"Jenna, my name is Dr. Saul. Tell me, what does my office smell like then?" he asked.

"It smells like spices and someplace far away. I don't recognize it, but that's okay." Then she mumbled to herself putting vowels and consonants together making clicking, nonsensical words and sounds.

My daughter and I sat back and listened as the doctor conversed with Jenna about everyday things, such as the concert that she claimed to have missed. After a half an hour of conversing, the doctor sent Jenna and I into the waiting room while he spoke to Camille alone. I gathered from the ghastly expression on Camille's face when she stepped out of the office that the news was not good. It was my turn to meet with the doctor; although I was not a parent, I was a guardian and primary caregiver. I was her grandmother.

"Your daughter will need support. She is in a state of shock at the moment, Shirley," the doctor said when I sat down across from him.

"Yes, Camille is already under a lot of stress with her demanding work schedule and honestly, this came on very suddenly," I confided.

"As it often does in these cases."

"May I ask you something? My grandmother was insane, she spent a stretch of time at Willard Hospital as a young woman. Can this be hereditary?"

"Certainly it can. It would be most helpful to me if I could obtain her medical records, do you have access to them?" he asked.

"I don't, but that's not to say I can't try to obtain them for you. I have memories that may be helpful and I am more than willing to share any information I can remember if it helps my granddaughter."

"Yes, she will need all the help she can get. I am sending her home because she is not harming anyone right now. She may seem confused at times, which is normal for what she is experiencing. You may notice swift mood swings, or changing sleep patterns and I ask you to jot down what you observe. We will meet regularly from now on and keep a sharp eye on her progression."

"Dr. Saul, what is the diagnosis?"

"It appears she has a psychotic disorder of some kind. It is even possible she might be having a psychotic break. However, until we have her tested for epilepsy, brain tumors, or encephalitis, we can't confirm this. We need to rule out any other medical conditions, or neurological disorders that involve the central nervous system."

"Oh my." I gulped in air, closed my eyes and felt the expansion of my lungs.

"Shirley, are you all right?" the doctor asked.

"Yes, I'm fine. Please go on," I answered.

"Once this testing is complete and we have more concrete information, we can go forward with a diagnosis. Psychotic disorders are most often diagnosed in teenagers or young adults, but it's not entirely uncommon to have an adolescent child present with these symptoms. Unfortunately, we have found that the younger a child is when they present with the classic symptoms, the more severe the case is."

The tears welled up in my eyes as I listened to the doctor.

"What can we do, doctor?" I said clutching the tissue he handed me.

"Be patient, be strong for your daughter, and we will meet again next week to discuss Jenna's CAT scan results."

"Thank you, Dr. Saul."

"You are welcome, and if anything else unusual comes up, don't hesitate to call me." He handed me his card, with his personal cell phone penciled in the corner.

His office made the necessary appointments for Jenna and now, all we could do was wait. My daughter took the week off from work, which would drastically affect her income, but it was imperative she be present for Jenna's testing.

The CAT scan was imposing and while we didn't tell Jenna precisely what kind of test she was getting, she grew uncomfortable when our car turned into the hospital parking lot. After we checked Jenna in, she was instructed to undress and put on a hospital gown that opened in the back. She seemed suspicious of the nurse who took her vitals and attempted to run an intravenous line in her arm. Jenna started talking quickly in gibberish: the nurse looked at my daughter and me questioningly but didn't say a word. The nurse found a vein and rubbed the spot with an alcohol swab. Jenna clicked her tongue and grew irritable but remained still while the needle was inserted. I wondered what she was thinking when she stared at the ceiling so intently.

Once the line was placed, she was transferred into an adjoining room and laid on a narrow table. Jenna shielded her eyes from the bright lights and looked uncomfortably at the sterile equipment surrounding us. While we waited for the head technician to arrive, Jenna grew restless and fidgety. She began tugging at her tape and tried ripping out the IV needle. She stood up to leave, claiming everyone in the room was out to get her. Her monologue became panicked and she started sweating on her brow.

"Jenna, everyone here is trying to help you. They just have to run some tests to determine your condition," I said calmly to my granddaughter. I placed a gentle hand on her shoulder, trying to force her back down to the cot. My daughter stood uncomfortably in the corner watching everything unfold.

"They put something in my brain, Grandma, through the needle in my arm and now they want it back. Don't let them hurt me, they want to kill me!" Jenna was sweating more profusely now and continued her attempts to try to flee. A large black man blocked the doorway and two nurses escorted her back to the cot, where her arms and legs were put in restraints.

Jenna screamed and clicked her tongue, her language strange and confusing to all of us who were around her. I tried to console her but her eyes were wide with fear. When the technician finally entered the room, he had a doctor with him. Jenna was administered a sedative via the IV to calm her so that the testing could take place. Everyone in the room was on edge, but my daughter was mortified.

The blood work and urine culture came back negative. Similarly, the results from the x-rays and CAT scans were normal; Jenna had no problems with her endocrine or metabolic systems.

This pointed to the fact she did indeed have a neurological or mental disorder. Dr. Saul phoned my daughter at home and scheduled an appointment for us with a pediatric neurologist the following day. This doctor was a close colleague of Dr. Saul's and he was able to make room for us in his schedule.

Jenna was reluctant to get out of bed the following morning. Camille and I had to drag her into a steaming hot shower to wake her up. Neither of us could get her to use soap or to wash her hair, Jenna feared the substances were poisoned. She dressed with great apprehension and tried lying back in bed, but we urged her to get ready for the day and promised her pizza for lunch. I felt like she was unraveling before my eyes.

The neurologist had a thick foreign accent that was hard to decipher and it made Jenna wary. She warmed up to his nurse, however, during her hearing and vision testing and the remainder of the tests ran smoothly. The exam was straightforward and the doctor was able to assess Jenna's motor and sensory skills, along with her speech and balance. He used a reflex hammer to check her nerves and a flashlight to study her eye movement. The exam only took half an hour and when we finished, we went straight to Dr. Saul's office. The neurologist told us he would call Dr. Saul with his results immediately.

The doctor's door was ajar when we arrived at his office; thankfully, this meant we didn't have to wait. We entered together and took seats as the doctor stood to greet us before closing the door. Jenna squeezed her eyes tightly shut when the door latched shut, her body tensed.

"I understand, Jenna, that you were uncomfortable with yesterday's testing?" Jenna just shrugged, fearful this doctor was out to get her as well.

"Well, the testing came back negative as you know. Jenna does not have any medical basis for her behaviors. I just spoke with the neurologist as well, and those tests were also negative. In other words, Jenna doesn't have any diseases that might present with speech deficiencies or mood swings. Having this information allows us to move forward with therapy to arrive at a diagnosis."

"Doctor, what are you looking for exactly?" I asked, while my daughter sat by, unusually quiet, holding Jenna's hands.

"This diagnosis will be tricky. I have ruled out Post Traumatic Stress Disorders, because she hasn't had any traumatic events or accidents."

Suddenly Jenna stood up. "You don't know me, you are just like the rest of them!" She yelled as she stormed from the room, slamming her fist against the wall on her way out. My daughter followed her outside and the doctor motioned that I allow them to retreat.

"She is displaying delusions of persecution. As you have just witnessed, she thinks people are out to get her. This is a common occurrence in schizophrenic patients. Jenna may even accuse you of being against her."

"Okay. Are you saying that my granddaughter has multiple personalities? The Jenna I know would never act like that. She has never had a violent bone in her body."

"No. Multiple personality disorder is quite different from schizophrenia. I can't say with one hundred percent accuracy that she is schizophrenic. It is possible she has another personality that is trying to come out, or she could have a mood disorder known as bipolar. If she is bipolar she could be displaying a manic episode at the moment, but only time can tell if this is the case. However, the licking, sniffing, and language are not normally indicative of bipolar disorder. At home, I need you to observe Jenna. If she continues to be irritable and accusatory, and restless, followed by extreme fatigue, withdrawal, and depression, I need to know. If her changes are less subtle, then that provides me vital information as well. Diagnosing children with mental illness is very tricky and takes time."

"Of course, I will keep an ongoing record."

"Also, it would be helpful if you can attend support groups in order to learn as much as possible about mood disorders. There you will learn what to look for and how to recognize behaviors that point to acute episodes." He handed me a pamphlet with information for a local support group for families with members who were mentally ill. The group met weekly in an open forum in a church basement in DeWitt.

"Will she ever be normal again?" I asked, biting the inside of my cheek and tasting the tangy blood.

"Jenna is being treated early which is good. I have every reason to believe she will respond to therapy and medication with support. Jenna sees the world differently than you and I. She appears to be having a break with reality, and she may hear or see things that don't exist. You have heard the odd language she uses; this is classic schizophrenic behavior. Often these patients create their own clipped words that make no sense to anyone else. Because Jenna feels like others are trying to harm her, she is slightly paranoid. Just reassure her that she is okay. Try to bring her back to the present using smells and sounds that are familiar and comforting. Sing a lullaby she was fond of as a child, bake cookies, or do something else that engages her."

"I can do that."

"Our approach to her care is gentle and conservative. We will try therapy alone first and see what results we achieve, if we are able to manage her outbursts, delusions, and language we will stay on course and hope for a full recovery. If she continues to develop further symptoms, if another personality evolves, or if she becomes a danger to herself, we will need to start medication.

All of our efforts are put in place so that she can be a functioning member of society."

"I understand."

"You mentioned a grandmother with mental illness, if you can get her records I would very much like to have a look at them. Sometimes this helps when diagnosing a patient."

"I will do my best. Willard Hospital closed in 1995 but I will make some calls."

"Very well then. Thank you for coming in with your daughter and Jenna, I can tell they need you."

I felt a weight bearing upon my shoulders and stood to leave, inhaling deeply as I left to find my family. I would feel better if we had a concrete diagnosis, but I understood the challenges Dr. Saul faced when observing Jenna.

CHAPTER NINETEEN

MEDICAL RECORDS

Willard Hospital closed in 1995, this much I already knew. I had thought a lot about my grandmother, Iona, over the years but until now, I didn't have a concrete reason to go digging around her past. My mother, Suzette, told me Iona spent a short period of time at this hospital when she was a young lady for being delusional and disobedient. I knew all about Hetty, because we had a framed sketch of her hanging above the mantle in our family room growing up and sometimes I saw Grandma talking to her. Given what we knew, it made sense to me that Iona was delusional. The rest of my grandmother's story, however, was a mystery. What happened to my grandmother during her confinement? How was she diagnosed and treated both medically and physically? Insane asylums had horrible reputations for mistreating their patients in the 1900s and I could only imagine what my grandmother was subjected too.

I Googled Willard Hospital and was met with an onslaught of information and photographs. Images of abandoned brick buildings with shattered windows and boarded up houses were scattered across dozens of websites. There were photographs of numerous bathtubs, stained with rust, positioned side by side and surrounded by the peeling paint from the once sea green walls. Wooden tranquilizing chairs with neck braces were centered in large desolate rooms. The scathing imagery sent shivers up my spine. More photos portrayed empty beds in dark hollow rooms. The photographs evoked images of fear and isolation.

Some websites had pictures that focused on the patients themselves. There were women labeled as "patients shown working in sewing rooms" while other patients were photographed enjoying the outdoors playing shuffleboard. Naked, feeble-minded women who indeed looked insane, could be found next to photos of female patients who were clean, well dressed, and looked normal by any standards. I wondered which of these categories my grandmother would have fit into. Was she disheveled and helpless, or did she care about her appearance and keep herself groomed?

Photos of women's and men's shoes, boots, and even wooden prosthetics could be found. Similarly, hairbrushes, curling irons, and other items for grooming were evident. Decks of cards and photo albums were displayed alongside photos of other means of entertainment. Steel film reels and a cinema room with lists of the movies shown on concurrent dates were on several different websites, as was the infamous Hadley Hall, the place where patients found amusement in the form of theater and games. Patients partaking in activities such as bowling were then followed up with ghostly images of empty lanes with fallen pins and balls.

Perhaps most troubling was the photograph of an empty morgue with tools strewn about, one tool had a deep curvature at its tip that was reminiscent of an ice cream scoop. I wondered immediately if lobotomies were performed at this institution and suddenly felt sick to my stomach.

Interestingly, images of Willard's patients' suitcases were all over the web. Over four hundred such suitcases were discovered deep within the recesses of a building's attic. It appeared the suitcases were stored in one particular building for decades and forgotten about. A group of researchers took it upon themselves to study and catalog the suitcases, and went so far as to have them documented on film.

The suitcases had the original contents still inside them. One lady's suitcase had syringes and bottles of medicine including laxatives, while another had toiletries and a sewing kit. Some individuals had novels and family photographs and others had Bibles and musical instruments. One woman had fourteen pieces of luggage that included furniture. Dozens of medical bags were found as well, which I thought was peculiar.

I wondered if my grandmother were in any of these images, or if her suitcase was found among the others. It was an interesting angle, and the more research I did, the more I became determined to go to an exhibit and find out.

One of the more informative websites led me to a phone number that I could call for information regarding patients who once resided at Willard. I placed a phone call in order to start the ball rolling and get Iona's medical records released. Numerous forms needed to be filled out; first and foremost, we had to prove we were related to an individual patient at Willard.

CHAPTER TWENTY

SHAME

 My daughter, Camille, and I quickly learned how shameful it was to have a beloved family member diagnosed with a mental illness. Aunts and uncles, cousins and distant relatives called out of concern, but when we elaborated on Jenna's condition and possible diagnosis, they became outraged and defiant. My daughter, Helen, was irate that her sister, Camille, would agree to take her daughter, her pride and joy, to therapy. "It just wasn't something we did," she said.

"If anyone finds out Jenna is in therapy, she'll never have friends. They'll think you guys are weird and she'll become a loner for life," Helen admonished.

"Helen, with all due respect, that's not your decision to make," Camille told her sister.

"I just saw that little pixie six months ago, and she was fine," Helen retorted.

"Well, things change quickly I guess," Camille said.

"Did you ever think it could be hormones? I mean all kids get wacky when they go through puberty and I noticed she was developing, if you know what I mean, last time we were there."

"It's more than that, Helen. If you'd just listen to me, you might understand," Camille pleaded with her sister.

"No, nope, I don't want to hear it. My niece is fine. She is not a schizoid, nor is she mental. The only one I question is you."

Helen was clearly not capable of being supportive. She was uninformed and ignorant. She shunned the idea that anyone in her family could suffer from mental illness. She had heard the stories about Iona, but that's all they were, stories. Luckily, the kids went to different schools, because her boys were similar in age to Jenna and Helen didn't want word to get around. She hated the thought of her boys being any less popular than they already were because of an awful rumor.

"Helen, I have to go." My daughter hung up the phone, but not before Helen told her to call when Jenna was all better.

"Mom, she doesn't have the flu, or a broken bone. Helen thinks if she has something wrong, there is an easy fix. Is everyone so ignorant?" Camille asked with tear-filled eyes.

"I sure hope not. I guess it's just not easy for them to understand or accept. Listen, we do have to talk about school." I said.

"I know. The principal called again. He suggested that we arrange for a tutor and see how it goes. If Jenna does well, we can finish off the year so she doesn't fall behind," Camille explained.

"I can move in here for a while, you know, to help. You have to work and I don't mind, I really don't. I can take Jenna to the library to meet her tutor and we can meet you for therapy," I offered.

"Yes, I suppose we'll have to work something like that out. She can't be left alone, that's for sure," my daughter agreed.

Before Jenna's well-being took a turn for the worse, we had a firm schedule in place. There was, however, one afternoon where Jenna was alone for the space of three hours. Somehow, during that time she left the house, took a bus to the mall, and wandered around alone. The mall security guard picked her up because she was acting oddly in the food court. She was irrational, and crouching in a corner, screaming that everyone in the mall was out to get her. She scratched the guard when he tried to retrieve her. He was unable to talk her down from her agitated state so he called the police.

When the police arrived, Jenna was unable to give them her private information. She couldn't recite her name or address and became increasingly volatile. She recited gibberish and sequestered herself further into the corner, crouching down with her knees to her chest. She pulled a dining chair in front of her to help her stay hidden.

Luckily, a neighbor was out shopping and recognized Jenna. She called Camille and we intervened just in time. If we hadn't arrived when we did, she would have been taken into custody. I coaxed Jenna out from her position and Camille spoke with the guard. She also talked with our neighbor and thanked her for calling, although she gave no explanation for Jenna's odd behavior. If the neighbor thought she was on LSD that would be okay. That might be a lesser offense than having a mental illness.

My daughter, Jenna, and I went for therapy as a family and individually in an attempt to understand how to move forward given Jenna's condition. The doctor diagnosed Jenna with schizophrenia and cautioned us that it could become more acute. After witnessing this incident, I became all too aware that Jenna's safety was at risk.

I had to be with her at all times and moved my things in to my daughter's small three-bedroom house at once. When Helen insisted on coming over for a visit, Jenna didn't recognize her. She lashed out at her and claimed she was an intruder from above and that she was sent to kill her. Jenna grew violent and punched and kicked Helen in an effort to protect herself. She tried running from the house, but I was able to stop her. I threw myself on top of her and waved Helen to leave.

"See, she's gone now. She won't hurt you."

"Okay."

"Do you think I would let anyone hurt you? You're my one and only granddaughter. What do you say we go bake some cookies?"

We went into the kitchen and made a double batch of triple chocolate chip cookies. Jenna measured and stirred the dry ingredients while I prepared the wet ones. We took turns mixing the batter and we scooped spoonfuls of the dough onto cookie sheets. For a fleeting moment, everything seemed normal. Jenna wasn't speaking gibberish, she looked at me when we talked, and she wasn't behaving paranoid or neurotic. She was at peace in my presence and I felt the need to protect her at all costs. Helen would have to stay clear from our home for a while, no surprise visits from anyone would be allowed.

The day the tutor was scheduled to meet us at the library, Jenna was particularly troubled. She went back and forth between outfits. I didn't care what she wore, I was merely grateful she showered and used soap. She wanted to please me for some reason and pleaded with me to help her decide on a shirt. When I picked a polka dot blouse that had once been a favorite, her eyes grew dark and stormy. She rushed from her room and stormed in to the bathroom. She slammed and locked the door and refused to come out. After an hour, I canceled the tutorial session and called Dr. Saul.

The doctor felt Jenna was experiencing more frequent, more acute, psychotic episodes that warranted intervention. If I couldn't coax her out of the bathroom, the doctor suggested that I call 911. I was fearful because we kept numerous prescription and over-the-counter medications in the cabinet. If Jenna was at all suicidal, all she had to do was swallow them. She was so unpredictable these days, and it wasn't just the paranoid outbursts. She was angry one minute and serene the next, one day she was relaxed and I was able to connect with her, but the next she would act like she didn't know me. It was frightening and I felt at a loss.

I was unable to pry Jenna from the bathroom and when Camille came home from work, she couldn't either. In the end, we called 911 and sat by silently as the team of experts unhinged the bathroom door and carried my listless granddaughter to an ambulance. Jenna had taken a variety of pills; I couldn't conceive that she was suicidal and had to believe it was this other, more sadistic side of her that acted when she popped the tops to the cabinet's medications and drained every last capsule.

Jenna was taken to the hospital where her stomach was pumped, then she was admitted to Hutchings Psychiatric Center at once. The weather in Syracuse was rainy and gray, like my heart. I felt tired and overwhelmed by the onslaught of events since the beginning of the school year. My once sweet and caring granddaughter had become an unrecognizable being. My daughter was in pieces and had been prescribed anti-anxiety medication to help her cope. She gained weight as a result and was always beating herself up about it.

The neighbors knew we had a situation thanks in part to the mall incident, but also because of the ambulance and squad of police cars that had stormed into our driveway last week. If they noticed that I moved in, they didn't mention it. In fact, they tried to pretend nothing was wrong. No one really pried, they just ignored us from that point on. We were weird, had a situation, and no one wanted to be involved.

Helen, God bless her, called us numerous times in tears. Her concern for her boys grew. Word had gotten out about Jenna and she didn't want them to suffer any teasing. Helen behaved selfishly, she really couldn't understand the ways in which Jenna was being tormented and she didn't try. I offered to take her to a meeting with me, but she refused. She didn't want to be seen entering "one of those meetings," so I went alone, again.

Listening to people speak about who their loved ones used to be before the disease of mental illness took over was the most distressing. I took my pleasure in the small moments when Jenna was back. I visited with her every day at Hutchings. In those small fractured moments, I might catch Jenna's eyes looking directly into mine with love. Sometimes she appeared confused and afraid, but more often she was in a world of her own, split off from reality.

"I have diagnosed Jenna as having schizophrenia," Dr. Saul said to us during one of our private therapy sessions. "I'd like to try an atypical anti-psychotic medication for her called Clozapine. I believe it will help her to be emotionally expressive and motivated at the same time. Like all medications it can have side effects, in this case weight gain is the most noted."

"Join the club," Camille said sarcastically.

I don't know what was harder for my daughter, seeing her child in an institution such as this one, or dealing with the outside population who didn't understand. There was a stigma to mental illness, it was shameful to admit to it or discuss it with anyone. Helen begged us not to tell anyone what was going on, but I thought that was ridiculous. Anyone who was a real friend would understand, wouldn't they?

CHAPTER TWENTY-ONE

RELEASE FORMS

The Authorization for Release form OMH-11 was not too difficult to obtain. I contacted the office of mental health and downloaded the necessary paperwork in duplicate. Dr. Saul was required to show that we had a demonstrable need for the information in the medical file we wanted released. The information in the files was deemed confidential by the HIPAA laws as well as the New York State Hygiene Law. Once the form was filled out, witnessed, and signed by the doctor and myself, we submitted it and crossed our fingers. Not only would Iona's file help inform of us of our family history but it would also help us with insurance. The costs to keep Jenna at Hutchings were unmanageable for us for much longer. Our insurance company noted that our costs exceeded the norm and refused to reimburse us for any care. Our only other option was to send her to a facility that was quite a distance away, and we felt that would be more traumatizing.

"Why don't we bring her home, Camille? We can monitor her meds as closely as the staff at Hutchings."

"I was thinking the same thing. She seems to be doing well on the current dosage, at least the staff hasn't indicated she's had outbursts."

"We can discuss it at therapy today. Who knows, maybe she won't want to come home?"

"I know, but the idea is to admit patients for a short period of time, not indefinitely. I just worry because she's really been distant the last few visits. It makes me so sad." Camille started crying. I held my daughter close and soothed her by rubbing her hair. I cried alongside her, spilling the tears I had been holding in for the last few weeks.

"It's going to be all right, Camille. She is in good hands, the best. I have written for Iona's files and we will learn more about our history. If Iona, my very own grandmother, went on to have a normal life, there is no reason to think Jenna can't."

"Times were much simpler then though, Mom. People are just so judgmental and I don't know, I wish we could all just go away and live away from the prying eyes."

"Why don't you come to a meeting with me this week? I have found it very helpful and I think you will too," I encouraged.

"I don't have time, I'm thinking of picking up an extra shift at work to make ends meet."

"Let me cash in my retirement, I'd rather do that than have you working anymore. You'll run yourself right into the ground and we need you."

"Mom, no, that's your money. We'll figure it out."

Later when we were at our therapy appointment with Dr. Saul and Jenna, we both noted that Jenna was more composed. She said hello and gave us both warm embraces. Her hair was brushed, she smelled like she'd had a fresh bath, and other than the sniffing and occasional glances to the ceiling, she seemed normal.

"Doctor, is there a possibility we could bring Jenna back home with us?"

"She's just settling into a nice routine here, I am not sure I want to interrupt her treatment and progress just yet."

"Could we try it? If she doesn't do well, we can return her.

Our health insurance isn't covering her care and we are running low on funds."

"I see. There are other federally funded facilities you could consider if you'd like."

"No, we would rather she came directly home so we can care for her."

"Well, let me discuss it in private with Jenna. If she agrees, we will establish some parameters. We don't like the patients to stay too long here, often we get them on track and to a place where we feel they aren't going to be harmful to themselves or anyone else. Jenna did attempt suicide once already so I have to be confident she is not depressed before I let her go. The medication is very effective and is doing its job, Jenna is more social now and has better control. She is also more aware of her surroundings and reality."

"We will be in the waiting room then."

Camille and I sat for a lengthy twenty minutes while Dr. Saul evaluated Jenna with a series of questions. When he was done, he determined she was not at risk for suicide. We were all in agreement that Jenna would come home with us at the end of the week. Dr. Saul wanted to continue to observe her for a few more days before her release.

Back home, Camille and I removed anything we saw that could be a potential trigger. In Jenna's case, mirrors acted as a trip wire for her. For some reason, they made her very sad. We removed every mirror in the house, including those in the main bathrooms. The only one we kept was in Camille's closet, it was a full length mirror, one of the cheap ten dollar ones from Target.

We replaced the mirrors with cheery photographs and inspirational quotes. We paid special attention to the items in Jenna's bedroom, placing her favorite books on her nightstand and a diary with lock beside it as well. Journaling was a tool utilized at Hutchings so we bought a purple, leather-bound, lined journal with a large cursive 'J' on the cover for this purpose.

When the day came to bring Jenna home, Camille and I were hopeful. Jenna was cheerful when we picked her up and seemed grateful to be back home and in familiar surroundings. She poured herself a glass of milk, plopped onto the couch, and settled in with her regular programs. We hadn't given up on a tutor just yet, but planned to wait a week or more to get Jenna comfortable before introducing someone new. Helen asked to come visit but we declined for now. Instead, we interested Jenna in cooking with us, we scrapbooked, and surprised her with a kitten.

Jenna adored her new pet. She named her kitten Mellow and took excellent care of her, feeding her and keeping her litter-box clean. She dangled yarn for hours while Mellow played with the skeins and she allowed her to sleep with her every night. We let her out occasionally, our yard was fenced and the fresh air did everyone good. Unfortunately, the kitten was small enough to fit through our fence posts and on one sunny afternoon, she ran away. We waited several days, but when she still hadn't returned, we lined the streets with "lost kitten" posters that had her photograph and our phone number.

Weeks went by and Mellow never returned. Jenna fell deeper into herself and rarely came out of her room anymore. When she did, it was merely to lay in a fetal position on the couch and watch television. We offered to bake, take walks, or go for car rides to get her mind on something else. We even suggested that we go Christmas shopping, but Jenna was uninterested. When we suggested we get a new kitten, Jenna stopped talking altogether. Dr. Saul was kept abreast of the situation and suggested we return Jenna to Hutchings for a brief stay. He was worried she was becoming depressed and suicidal once more.

We coaxed Jenna back to Hutchings where she quickly assimilated to the routine. She remained speechless and withdrew even further into herself, if that was possible. Her listlessness concerned the doctor.

"I have discussed Jenna's case with the assisting doctor. He suggested ECT therapy for Jenna. I want to explain it in detail to you before we make any decisions."

"Oh my goodness, electric shock is barbaric, how could you even suggest that, Dr. Saul?" Camille asked through her tears.

"It used to be barbaric, you are correct. Patients were not given sedatives or anesthesia before being lined up for blasts of ECT. They were shocked repeatedly and often died. Today ECT is extremely safe and reliable, especially for cases like this. Patients who are not responding to conventional therapy and medication are given ECT as a means to accelerate the benefits of medication. In my experience, depressed patients, in particular, have rapid clinical improvement as a result of the procedure."

"Can't we just try a different medication?"

"We certainly could, however, I don't want to waste time and risk stepping backwards. Jenna was showing signs of improvement, but she had an incident that sparked her decline. If we can accelerate the medications, it will be highly beneficial to everyone involved, and I promise you there is no risk of injury."

"So how does electric shock therapy get administered nowadays?" I asked.

"Good question, Shirley. We start by giving the patient muscle relaxants or anti-anxiety medication to relax them and get them ready for the procedure. We insert an IV so that we can administer an anesthetic. Both medications serve to protect the patient from injuring themselves and our staff. Small electrodes are attached to the scalp and seizures are induced with the electric stimuli. Seizures last from twenty-five to thirty seconds.

The technique will be administered two to three times per week. Normally, a series of twelve procedures is given over a course of three weeks. In Jenna's case, I would opt for a four-week course, starting with two treatments and increasing as necessary."

"What are the side effects of this, Dr. Saul?" Camille asked.

"As with any medical procedure, the patient runs the risk of reacting adversely to the anesthetic used. This would be extremely rare, but it has happened. Also, extremely rare would be cardiovascular complications, or oral complications. As I said earlier, she will not be in any pain or discomfort, but she may feel confused or have a headache afterward. Some patients have a brief period of memory loss, or feel nauseous. In my professional opinion, I do feel it is worth the risk. Jenna is at a pivotal point in her treatment. I would strongly urge you to go home and think it through, discuss it with each other, and call me with any questions."

We asked to visit with Jenna before we left and were led into a group room where Jenna was sitting watching television. She slouched on the sofa, hugging her knees and averting her eyes away from us. She talked to herself in the language only she knew and hardly noticed when we left. Screams and sobs from other sick patients echoed through the hallway and rang in my ears.

"What did I do wrong, Mom?" Camille asked me on the way home. I pulled the car over, and turned off the ignition.

"You did nothing wrong, this is like any other disease. Can a person help it if she gets diabetes or cancer? Those are also genetic and can be treated with medications, medical procedures, and therapy too. This is not any different. You have to stop thinking this is your fault or you will drive yourself crazy."

"If I had been around more, maybe I could have done something to stop it."

"I don't think mental illness can be prevented, Camille, and she is predisposed. If anyone is to blame, it's me. It was my grandmother after all that was mentally ill, so it was in my genes. I am sorry for that, I really and truly am."

"That's like saying you're sorry I was born, and I am grateful for my life. I am just so overwhelmed by all of this, Mom, I don't know if I can handle it."

"I thought you were feeling better over the last few weeks, do you think your anti-anxiety medicine is working?"

"It was helpful at first, but now I don't know. Sometimes I feel like it just masks my emotions and I don't want that. Other times it gives me the energy I need to face the day. I am planning to stay on it for now even though I have gained fifteen pounds."

"We both talked about getting more therapy too, outside of Dr. Saul. Maybe that would help? Doesn't your insurance cover that at least?"

"It does. It just takes more time from my day and I have so little to spare as it is."

"Well, I cashed in a portion of my retirement. It'll get us by for the next six months or more if we play our cards right. I think we should grab a pizza for tonight, and maybe think on the ECT procedure, how does that sound to you?"

"Pizza sounds great. ECT for my little girl, not so great."

CHAPTER TWENTY-TWO

ECT

Camille and I researched and talked at length about ECT treatment as an option for Jenna. After several discussions with the doctor as well, we finally agreed that it was time to try it.

We explained to Jenna what was going to happen, as did the doctor. Jenna kept her gaze elsewhere during our visits and rocked her body back and forth in our presence. We never really knew what she heard anymore and had no idea what she was thinking.

"Jenna, today is your first treatment," I said to my granddaughter as I walked into her room. I sat on her bed and reached over to take her hand in mine. Her mom followed behind me. I sensed her agitation immediately and the floor nurse suggested it had to do with her breakfast schedule being altered. She was not allowed to eat or drink anything for twelve hours before the shock treatment and this put her in a dizzying state. She paced the wooden floors of her small bedroom and talked animatedly to herself all the while.

"Time to go," said the unfamiliar nurse who appeared at Jenna's doorway with a wheelchair. She interrupted Jenna's pacing and expertly maneuvered her into the chair. When the foot pedals were positioned, she proceeded to wheel her down a narrow corridor that was unfamiliar to me. The hallway wound around several corners, connecting the buildings, and led to the back building where the ECT treatments took place. Jenna was changed into a hospital gown and held down as the nurses tried to place the IV in her forearm. Confused and scared, Jenna lashed out and made the insertion very difficult. Finally, her favorite nurse, Barbara, was able to calm her enough so that another attending staff member was able to place the IV and administer the relaxant. She was strapped down to the table and small electrodes were placed on her scalp and chest. Soon after the sedative was administered, Jenna became sleepy and closed her eyes. I held her hand and Camille rubbed her hair. Then she was wheeled away from us and taken in to a specialized room for her first of a long series of treatments.

"Everything went well," Dr. Saul approached us in the waiting room. He was wearing hospital scrubs and a mask that he pulled over his head while we talked.

"Is she okay?" Camille asked.

"She has a headache and did throw up, which can be a side effect from the anesthesia. I doubt she remembers anything past the waiting room though."

"Will we see any results today? Is that possible?" I wondered out loud.

"It's possible but not likely. I expect to see improvements by the third or fourth treatment. So, in two days we will repeat what we did today, and then next week we will have two more series. After that, I might increase the intensity and go three times a week. That won't be determined just yet."

"Thank you, Dr. Saul. May we see her?" Camille was overcome with fear for her daughter and although the procedure was quick and painless, it didn't lessen her concern.

"The nurse will come out and get you once she is more lucid."

The first of many treatments was behind us now.

CHAPTER TWENTY-THREE

PHOTOGRAPHS

While we waited and prayed for Jenna to react to her treatments, I researched the suitcases that were left behind at Willard. I struck gold because there was going to be a presentation at the Ithaca Free Library in a few weeks. I fully intended to be at the presentation.

It could take several months to receive Iona's medical records, so we took the matter into our own hands and launched into a historical tour of our family. Maybe it didn't matter if anyone else was plagued with mental illness, but if they were it might help in Jenna's recovery process. We have been told multiple times that family members who share DNA do well on similar medications. Meaning, if we had a cousin or anyone else fighting a similar battle and they had already tried medications it could help narrow the choices for Jenna. Additionally, it could be helpful knowing we weren't alone.

"I know people don't talk about this stuff, but if one of the cousins has anything like Jenna, I for one would want to know. We could be a good support to one another," I said to my girls as we focused our efforts on the family tree we were making.

My daughters and I gathered and sifted through all the newspaper clippings and photographs we had of Iona and her family. We placed what we had in a large shoebox to catalog later. Helen was beginning to understand the toll Jenna's condition was taking on me and Camille and became more empathetic to our situation. She reached out to cousins and any living relatives to seek information, time lines, and pictures.

We drew a family tree on a large piece of poster board and tacked it right to the wall. The tree was not divided between Iona and James's families because we had no information whatsoever about James's kin. One photograph was of a portly farmer wearing overalls and sucking hay, but no one knew who the man was. Because the photograph was well-preserved we always assumed it was someone of importance to James, otherwise his family was a mystery. We focused our research on Iona and her children and set to work with a time-line.

Unlike James, Iona had some photographs that were revealing. Photos of herself as a youth depicted an unhappy, unsmiling child. She had perfect posture but was so thin that by today's standards she would be considered undernourished. In the photo I stared at now, my grandmother's hair was pulled tightly back with ribbon, making her eyes bulge out and appear like huge saucers. Her parents flanked her, but no one touched each other. There was no loving hand on a shoulder, no contact at all. In fact, you could see the wallpaper behind and between the folks in the photograph due to how far apart they stood. Iona appeared to be in her teen years when this photo was taken, we would guess around fourteen years of age. Until she was older and had a family of her own, we didn't find one other picture of her.

As an adult, Iona had several photos taken together with her family. The grouped family photos were of particular interest to me. I studied my grandmother, the woman perched on a chair, whose hair was long and graying. She didn't wear it up as so many women did during this time-period, instead, it hung in waves, past her shoulders, framing her face. She was a pretty woman, a natural beauty you could say. Her features were symmetrical and strong. Her nose was straight and pointed, but not overly sharp. Her eyes were almond shaped, with eyebrows that arched perfectly across them. She had deeply embedded crow's feet, and in the photos where she was smiling, she had all her teeth.

Her clothing was not fancy, but it was not dour or dowdy either. Instead, it was colorful and straightforward, as I envision her to be. In the photo where she was seated alone on the porch, one arm up and over the back of the chair, she seemed to be looking at someone who wasn't there.

The next picture was snapped with the entire family present and a baby was sitting on her lap. The baby had fiery red hair, and was sucking his two middle fingers. You could almost imagine the drool sweeping from chin to bib when studying him. Beside the baby an older boy stood, he was a toddler and I knew that was my Uncle Johnathan. The girl beside Uncle Johnathan was older, she has a letter "S" embroidered on her smock so I presumed this child was, Suzette, my mother.

The family looked happy and healthy in this photograph. There were other photos where a couple, labeled Ben and Jennifer, were surrounding the group. They may have been family members of James's but we would never know. However, one would deduce the couple was well loved. James himself was shown with both arms around the pair in more than one photo.

We were confused by the photo that Uncle Daniel's daughter, my cousin, Marlin, sent. The photo shows the same red-haired baby boy being held by a woman who was clearly not related. The woman was skeletal, her eyes frantic, her hair frayed. She wore a dress with stitching on the pocket that we could not make out. I think her hair could have been red, but Camille and Helen think it was brown. The age of the photo and the fact it was black and white made it hard to say for sure.

"We have to find out more about this picture. I swear it is the same baby boy, and I think that may be letters or numbers on her pocket," I said to Camille, pointing to the mystery woman's dress.

"We should take it to a specialist, Mom. I am sure we can find someone who repairs antique photos. Maybe they can even blow it up and we can get a better look at the image."

"Okay, let's put it aside for now and label it as needing further research."

"Done," Camille said as she cataloged the picture and then clipped it behind the family photo where the same child was sitting on Iona's lap.

We had spent days going through photos and categorizing them, when I found a single photo of a child named Lucy. This child was standing on her own two feet, holding a blanket. She wore a dress with smocking across the bodice and ruffled short sleeves. Her hair had been combed back and hung in waves just below her ears. This photo looked professionally done, it has been cropped and matted, while all the others appeared to be from a simple Kodak camera.

"Wow. The child in this picture bears a striking resemblance to Iona, yet I have no recollection of her. My mother never mentioned another child to me. It's odd, really odd. Put this in the research pile, dear," I said as I handed the mystery photo to Camille. Helen looked at it as well and suggested calling our cousin, Gi-Gi.

Gi-Gi was Johnathon's one and only child. The story goes that he and his wife struggled to get pregnant and had lost all hope when Gi-Gi was conceived. Gi-Gi was spoiled and doted on, causing quite a stir among the cousins. She bragged relentlessly about her newest hair combs, and finery, along with her books and the extravagant trips she took with her parents, making everyone else feel inferior.

When Gi-Gi married a banker, she fully expected to live a lavish life that resembled her upbringing. Instead, the buffoon she married invested their money in scheme after scheme, leaving them broke with two girls, Claire and Susan, to feed. Gi-Gi amazed everyone when she held her head high as her family moved from a four-bedroom home into an apartment complex. She began work as a secretary to earn a small income and help climb the family out from debt. However, when the banker was found with lipstick on his collar and started coming home drunk several times a week, Gi-Gi left the louse for good. She filed for divorce and was awarded sole custody of the girls.

Gi-Gi moved her girls into an even smaller apartment and vowed never to re-marry. Instead, she threw herself into a career at Kodak, working her way up the ladder becoming the first female executive in the company.

Gi-Gi stayed true to her word and never so much as dated again. She earned a substantial income at Kodak and retired with enough savings to allow her to remain comfortable the rest of her days. Currently at sixty-eight, she was enjoying good health and time home with her grandchildren.

"I got a call from Marlin today. She found a trunk full of her daddy's treasures that she said we could have. One of us just needs to go get them. She said it would cost an arm and a leg to mail, but that it has pictures and a bundle of letters too," Helen said.

"Well, geez, I can go to Maine and get them, but Camille, I'd hate to leave you alone for more than a few days," I said.

"Mom, I will be fine. It's a six-hour drive so you should stay on a while, take a break from all of this." She gestured to the table full of photos and the poster board as well.

"What if Jenna has a break through?" I asked.

"I will contact you right away if she does. Really, Mom, you deserve a break."

"All right, let me call Marlin and see if she is free next week." Truthfully, I wanted the break. I didn't enjoy long car rides anymore, but the beach and fresh ocean air could be reviving. I spent so much time focused on Jenna and Camille that I wasn't taking care of myself the way I should be. I had gained fifteen pounds over the course of six months and worried about my sugar levels. I had pre-diabetes and needed to take a time out.

CHAPTER TWENTY-FOUR

MARLIN

I packed a small bag for my trip to Maine. I was sure to include both of the photographs that included the baby boy in question. I hoped Marlin might have some insight as to who the woman holding him in the picture could be. I loaded my car with snacks and country music CDs and set off.

I hated leaving Camille alone, but thought she might enjoy some time to herself. We rarely, if ever, fought, but still it was nice to have the house all to yourself once in a while.

My drive was tedious, but when I crossed into the state of Maine, my heart fluttered. Maine was our vacation destination as children. My parents and their siblings would rent a small house a few blocks from the beach for two weeks every summer. During the stay, the cousins were able to form lasting bonds and the parents were able to unwind.

I rolled down my driver-side window and inhaled the salty sea air. Memories of scavenger hunts and long walks on the beach came flooding back to me. I was known as the family beachcomber, I spent hours every morning scouring the beach for sand dollars or sea glass. I still had my sea glass collection displayed in my apartment.

I arrived at Marlin's home in York, already feeling refreshed by the change of scenery. She made a fresh pot of seafood chowder because she knew it was my favorite. We ate our fill and caught each other up on family news. I explained to her in greater detail what was happening with Jenna and she was very saddened by our situation. Marlin never had biological children of her own, but could only imagine our distress. Marlin's brother, whom we fondly called Davey, had two boys, David Junior and Matthew. They each had two kids of their own. It was David Juniors son, Noah, that had his share of issues. Yet until now, I didn't understand their depth. Marlin explained to me that when Noah was seventeen years old he had horrible mood swings. They blamed hormones initially, but then they realized he was dealing with a deeper issue. He was diagnosed with bipolar depression.

"Was he treated as an out-patient?" I asked Marlin about her nephew.

"Yes, he was initially," Marlin cleared her throat before continuing.

"Uh-oh," I commented.

"He had an incident, where he was manic and uncontrollable. He was a danger to himself so he was admitted against his will. It was awful. Eventually, they fine-tuned his medications and he was sent home. I don't see a lot of him, but I think he still struggles. If Davey were alive to see it, he would be beside himself. He loved his boys with all his heart and wanted nothing but the best for them."

"That's what we all want. Camille is on medication now for anxiety. I mean, what is this world coming to? They didn't have all this medication back when Iona was at Willard."

"No, they didn't. Back then they just took out a part of patient's brains and crossed their fingers for the best."

"Can you imagine?" I asked.

"I can't. Oh, goodness, I almost forgot to show you this. Hold on..."

Marlin disappeared, but when she came walking back into the kitchen she had a drawing of Hetty. It was different from the one that hung in my house growing up, but it was Hetty all right. She had a very distinct look, those apple-shaped cheeks, the full face, double chin, dimple, and ample bosom couldn't be mistaken.

"Wow, that's different from mine. Yours is even labeled." At the bottom of the drawing Hetty's name was spelled out.

"Iona was able to live with her demons, so why can't the rest of the world?"

"Well, Jenna simply can't. She isn't capable half the time." I grew misty thinking of my granddaughter and explained to Marlin the lengths that I was going to in order to obtain Iona's medical records. I also told her about the traveling suitcase exhibit and she thought that sounded rather interesting.

"The exhibit is in Ithaca next week. I have already contacted the gentleman who took the photographs and he has agreed to meet with me before his presentation."

"That could be very productive. It would be incredible to think Iona's suitcase could be among those found."

"I don't want to get my hopes up, but that would be insightful to say the least."

Marlin and I pulled out the trunk she had inherited from her father, Daniel, who was Iona's youngest son. She admitted it had been stored in her attic for over twenty years now and that she had never taken the time to go through it. The contents were musty and irrelevant at the time. Now, however, the case was important, so we started taking the items from the trunk one at a time. In it, we found more photos of the mystery woman. She was always frazzled looking and always wore an unappealing, droopy gray dress with numbers on the pocket.

"Do you think she was an inmate somewhere?" Marlin asked.

"I'm not sure. Why else would she have numbers on her pocket?"

"Do you suppose patients had numbers to identify them? I mean, you have to admit she looks like a patient. She is so dazed and frail, sort of cuckoo if you know what I mean," Marlin stated.

Looking at the photos, I did know what she meant. The woman held the baby at length, like she was frightened of hurting him. She had the beginnings of a smile in one picture, but in all the others, she was stoic and defeated. Her hair indeed looked red in some of the photographs and it was always unkempt and knotted.

We continued to paw through the trunk and came upon a stack of letters. The letters were fading, but with a magnifier we could make them out.

The correspondence seemed to be between three women. We could easily make out Iona's name and were able to recognize her penmanship. We determined that another author of the letters was from a woman who claimed to be the godmother to the baby, Daniel. Her name was Jennifer and we questioned whether or not she was related. Finally, the last woman who had letters in the stack was named Cat. We presumed Cat was the frazzled woman in the photographs because her notepaper was stock paper, not stationery. We coded the letters and then arranged them chronologically. Marlin took half of the letters to read and I took what was left and we relayed our findings to one another.

"Holy smokes," I said after reading one of the letters in my group.

"What?" Marlin asked.

"Sit down. I don't know how to tell you this, cousin, but if what I just read is accurate, then we aren't biologically related." I put the magnifying glass on the table and sipped my tea. I stared into the distance, trying to make sense of what I'd just uncovered.

"What on earth are you talking about, of course we're related."

"According to these letters, this Cat woman, the frazzled looking one, is Daniel's biological mother. It appears that Iona adopted him because Cat was in trouble with the law. There are references to stealing horses, and even murder." I put my hand across my mouth and chewed my bottom lip. It was all making sense.

"Oh my," Marlin said, sipping her tea beside me.

"I recognize this Jennifer woman. We have a picture of her at home. She is standing with Iona and her family. They look to be very close, but I still don't think they are related. They look nothing alike and we know it isn't her mother. We have photos of her mother so that is certain. In the letters, Jennifer refers to Daniel as her godson. 'I am taking good care of my godson…' she says right here." I pointed to the place in the letter where Jennifer made the claim.

Marlin held the magnifying lens to the letter and surely it indicated that Jennifer was Daniel's godmother. It made sense too that Daniel was Cat's son; they were the only two with red hair in the family.

"Which explains a bit about my nephew's illness, he has a great-grandmother with mental illness too. My God."

"My God is right."

"I am going with you to the suitcase exhibit. Maybe this Cat woman has her belongings there too. If she does, they would rightfully belong to me. I mean, that would make her my grandmother."

I reached across the table and held tight to Marlin's hand, we would find the answers together.

CHAPTER TWENTY-FIVE

HANGING BY A THREAD

Marlin and I walked along Wells Beach from the public walkway down to the jetty. It was about one mile each way and felt invigorating. Just walking along the ocean was restorative. It always served to remind me how small we were in comparison to the world. That something larger was at work, and that while life wasn't always fair, it was beautiful if we knew where to look. Just then I saw a glimmer in front of me, I bent over to pick it up and sure enough, it was a blue piece of sea glass. I held the treasure and took a deep breath, for the road ahead was long.

Marlin packed and prepared to drive home with me. She would stay at my apartment where there was plenty of room for her to spread out. I called Camille ahead of time to prepare her and Helen, but Jenna was still an in-patient so we didn't have to worry about that.

I was getting anxious to be home. Camille had something to discuss with me but she didn't want to do it over the phone. I knew there was no change in Jenna's condition and wondered if the doctor wanted to increase her shock therapy.

The drive was smooth and we were home by mid-afternoon. Marlin hugged Camille and Helen tightly and when the group broke apart, there were tears all around. We sat down together and told the girls about our discovery. They were saddened and surprised to learn that Marlin wasn't our biological relative, but we decided collectively that we were family regardless. If anything, the discovery brought us closer together. Helen drove Marlin to my apartment giving me time to catch up with my daughter.

"How is she?" I asked, sitting down with my daughter.

"She is the same, Mom. The ECT is not going as well as Dr. Saul hoped it would. She hasn't had any incidents, but she isn't markedly improved either."

"It's only been a few days, though, so what does that mean, where do we go from here?" I asked.

"He brought up the idea of a half-way house. He said there are several in Syracuse that would fit Jenna's needs well. The cost of keeping her at Hutchings is just too much, and our insurance might cover the half-way house. I just don't know though, Mom. I would prefer that she were here being taken care of by people who love her. I just can't imagine her being happy among multiple caregivers who care more about a paycheck than the patient."

"Well, you can't say that would be true for all the caregivers. I am one hundred percent certain that Dr. Saul would not release her into the care of anyone who wasn't qualified."

"I know. I trust his judgment, I really do. It's just hard."

"What I want to know is how you are doing? How is Camille?"

"I am hanging on by a thread, Mom, and that's about all I can muster. I am just so sad for what my daughter is missing out on, and for what I am missing out on. I mean there was a school dance this week. If none of this had happened, we would have spent the week shopping and getting her all dolled up. Instead she is facing ECT treatments and living in a room with cinder blocks for walls," my daughter admitted through her tears.

"All we can do is have faith. Let's not give up yet, she may still be able to go to a dance in high school. Okay?" I pleaded, wiping her eyes with my sleeves.

"Okay." Camille answered, leaning into me for a hug.

We were interrupted by a phone call coming from Hutchings. It was Dr. Saul and he wanted to let us know that he received a package from the Office of Mental Health in Binghamton, New York. Iona's medical records had been unearthed at long last. They were sent to him directly because of the HIPAA laws that stated even though a patient was deceased, they still retained the right to patient confidentiality.

"Oh my goodness, it's the medical records. They are finally here," I said, holding Camille's hands in my own.

CHAPTER TWENTY-SIX

MORE MEDICAL RECORDS

"Her attending physician was a man by the name of Dr. Macy. It says that Iona became a patient in the year 1915 at the age of fifteen years old. She is initially described as being a frightened, malnourished, yet educated young woman with severe mental disturbances. For instance, upon her admittance she had a shaved head and was described by her parents as being unruly. After numerous psychotherapy appointments, she is diagnosed as having delusions of grandeur as well as having obsessive compulsive disorder. The doctor had noted that Iona's delusions had names, the first being Hetty. The second delusion was Rose Mary who Iona believed was another patient on her ward, although the notes indicate there was no such person. The documents detail Iona's obsession with counting and they detail the therapies she was treated with, namely the hydrotherapy baths. The hydrotherapy is notated as working to calm Iona's nerves. The notes state that she was involved, or had several scuffles with, another patient that ultimately got her placed on different ward, one that was more strict." Dr. Saul shuffled the papers and adjusted his glasses before continuing.

"She was employed at the facilities barn, working with the horses, and initially appears to do well in the position. Then Dr. Macy receives complaints that Iona is disturbing the other patients, he notes that she has become violent and has even resorted to theft. As a result, it is decided that at night time her wrists must be shackled to her bed posts and her room remain locked so that she cannot get out. He describes her room and personal hygiene as grave. She sleeps in her own fecal matter and urine, no longer brushes her hair or washes. The doctor has a notation that he is considering other forms of therapy such as insulin shock therapy or skull drills. The doctor notes that six months after her admittance, she falls gravely ill and is in quarantine for five days. She is diagnosed with the flu and taken care of in the infirmary. Then she disappears along with his horse. The last note indicates that several search parties were sent to locate the patient but that she was never found."

Dr. Saul closed the manila envelope with Iona's records and sipped his coffee. "The field of psychiatry has obviously advanced in the last century. Dr. Macy's definition and understanding of delusions of grandeur may have been a blanket diagnosis for a wide range of illnesses. However, because he describes her hallucinations in great detail, we can infer that she was schizophrenic. She didn't have some of today's classic symptoms that we look at when diagnosing a person with delusions of grandeur, in other words from what I can tell she didn't have fantastical beliefs about herself. She didn't think she was a queen with great wealth, or that she was all powerful. It's possible she had bipolar disorder that went undiagnosed. I say this because the images she saw are described as coming and going. If she were in a manic state for instance, she would have been more likely to see them all the time. Does that make sense?"

"It sounds like Jenna," I said.

"It certainly helps to have these records. Now we know for certain there is a genetic component. Unfortunately, because it was so long ago we don't have treatment options to use as a guide."

"What about the hydrotherapy? Is that still used today?" Camille inquired.

"When we think of hydrotherapy today we envision nice relaxing baths and calming music. However, back in the early 1900s the baths were altered based on the patient's constitution. In other words, if a patient was lethargic and unresponsive to any other therapy, they were treated with stimulating sprays or submerged for hours in ice-filled tubs. Some institutions practiced a procedure that involved wrapping the patient like a mummy in soaked towels and then submerging them in water. They were strapped tightly to the tub and blasted with high jet streams of water. Conversely, if a patient was hyperactive, they were given warm baths and often kept in the water for days at a time in order to subdue them. Today, all of this has been replaced with psychiatric medications which I believe work better and are more humane for the patient."

"It's hard to imagine my grandmother enduring such cruel treatment."

"Yes, I understand. However, doctors back then did their best to implement therapies that they believed worked. They didn't think they were in the dark ages, but using the most modern advances to help treat patients."

"Where do we go from here with Jenna? The ECT doesn't seem to be having much of an impact."

"We have to give it more time. Some patients take longer to react to the therapy and Jenna may be one of them. Have you discussed the half-way house situation yet?"

"Yes, briefly. It's difficult to imagine Jenna being under someone else's care when she could be at home with us."

"I understand. The house I have in mind for Jenna is located in Cazenovia. It is a co-ed facility for adolescents and has two full-time chaperones with nursing degrees who reside there.

There are eight children residing there with four aides at all times. There is twenty-four hour care by professionals. If you want to set up a tour, you may do so. Here is the phone number and the contact person." He handed us a piece of paper with the information scrawled across the top.

"We will do that."

"For the rest of the week, we will continue our current course of action and reassess her situation as necessary. We will get her stabilized before we make any big moves."

When Camille and I came home, Marlin was making phone calls of her own to the Mental Health Agency. She was interested in obtaining her grandmother Cat's records. She desperately needed information on the woman, and thought it might help her nephew as well. Records were not released unless there was a doctor who requested them, so Marlin put calls into her brother Dave's ex-wife. Their relationship was estranged but she prayed that the call would be returned.

In the meantime we prepared a list of questions for our meeting with Jon Crispin. Jon was the photographer who cataloged the suitcases that were found in storage after the Willard Asylum for the Insane closed in 1995 due to budgetary constraints. Our research indicated that the suitcases were found by a former employee who was tasked with emptying the old buildings of their contents. The woman, Beverly Courtwright, opened a door to the attic of one of the back buildings and among the cobwebs and debris, found racks of possessions and suitcases belonging to former patients.

Beverly contacted a curator at the New York State Museum and told him of her discovery. The curator, Craig Williams, then oversaw the collection of more than four hundred suitcases. The contents of each case were cataloged, and photographed. Then they were stabilized and placed in a collection at the museum.

It was not only possible, but also probable, that if Iona ran away, her belongings were left behind. While Jon's exhibit only included a small number of suitcases, he had access to the rest.

When the day of the exhibit arrived, we went early to Ithaca. We had lunch at the Ithaca Bakery and did a quick tour of Cornell University. Camille, Marlin, and I met with Jon an hour before his presentation.

"Thank you for meeting with us, Jon. We have obtained records for our family member, Iona, and we are praying her suitcase may be among the ones in your exhibit."

"Unfortunately, it isn't in my exhibit, I only have six with me today. However, the name rings a bell. Mind you, I photographed over four hundred suitcases, but I seem to recall the name Iona. If you have time today, after the exhibit I will call Craig Williams and have him check our records. If the suitcase was left behind, he would be the man to talk to."

"May we have it back, I mean if it's there?"

"I am not sure, you'd have to discuss that with Craig. Right now they are the property of the museum, but I suppose if you can prove it belongs to your family member, there is always the possibility they will release it to you."

"Wow. What an incredible discovery."

"You can say that again. It's been a humbling journey. I think it's incredibly important to share the collection of photographs with a wider audience in order to understand the human side of the disease of mental illness," Jon said.

"I agree, maybe it will help shed light on mental illness and how far we have come to understand it."

"Yes, and how far we still need to go," Camille added.

The presentation Jon gave was educational and well done. To gaze upon the belongings of people admitted to Willard Asylum and to learn about their life histories was thought provoking.

The dignity with which the time capsules were preserved was a testament to Jon and the interns who handled the contents. The suitcases differed greatly in their contents, offering a glimpse into the mind of the troubled patient who lived during a time when being different meant being isolated. Of tremendous interest was what the patient packed, or had packed for them. What the cases had inside described the patients more fully than any medical records could. Jon described the contents of several suitcases as examples. For instance, there was the woman who did beautiful needlework. There was the obsessive compulsive man whose notebook contained every single railway station in the United States. There was the gay military man and the leather worker. Most troubling was that the full names of the patients could not be revealed. This brought up the question as to whether or not this stigmatized the patients and their families further.

Jon opened the floor for discussion. He started by saying that "normal" can be a relative term. Much depended upon when and where you were born and who your family was. The discussion that ensued delved heavily into the subjective nature of what defines a human being as being mentally ill and then how they must be treated. The historical treatment of mental illness, and the use of restraints, along with sedatives and hypnotic agents in the past versus the medicated climate we live in today was examined. We discussed the ideology of the Prozac nation, and the fact that as a society, we were taking more and more pills to cure our problems. There were no right or wrong answers to the questions posed during the discussion, but it did serve to bring attention to the plight of mental illness.

After the discussion, Jon called Craig and we scheduled a meeting with him for the end of the week. We would travel to Albany and be taken to the viewing room of the collection.

CHAPTER TWENTY-SEVEN

SUITCASES

We arrived in Albany and went directly to the museum. Craig Williams set aside time so that he could personally meet with us and escort us to the suitcase collection. We were taken into a storage room that contained numerous shelves of musty smelling luggage. There were cases of all shapes and sizes. Some were in mint condition with straps and buckles that remained in working order. Others looked to be falling apart. As Craig directed us to the far right corner of the room, the ghostly remains of all that surrounded me sent a shiver down my spine.

Propped on its back side and opened before me was a small brown leather suitcase. Inside it were the contents that would presumably belong to a small girl. Neatly folded one on top of the other were nightgowns, underwear, socks, two skirts and their corresponding blouses. Beside them was a Bible, a decaying toothbrush, a hairbrush, and faded ribbon. There was a small sewing kit, two small needles and two spools of thread. There were no scissors. A pair of hand-knit indoor slippers sat on top of the clothing and a blanket was on top of the toiletries. Tucked in the side was a set of pretty stationery and a pen.

The name beside the suitcase read Iona Meuller. We had found my grandmother's belongings.

Overcome with emotion, I reached out to touch my grandmother's personal effects. Craig caught my hand and asked that I only look at the objects. The items weren't meant to be disturbed and I understood that. He showed me photographs of each item individually and offered to make copies as well.

"May we have the suitcase, Craig?" I asked boldly.

"It's interesting, Shirley, years ago we tried to track down family members of the patients so that the cases could be claimed. However, in most cases no one was interested. Either the patient was such a blight on the family that succeeding generations didn't know of their existence, or family members had died. I will put your request in writing and discuss it with the board. I believe you should have this. However, it is part of a collection now, and an important part of our history."

"Yes, but looking at the other suitcases, Iona's is so simple. She doesn't have anything really personal inside. It looks like she didn't pack it herself," I said.

"I would concur. It was most likely packed by her mother. If a fifteen year old child packed it I would expect to see a different assortment of items, maybe a doll or some trinkets and a diary. Not necessarily sewing needles and thread."

"It certainly gives us a lot to think about and discuss. Thank you, Craig, for handling a piece of our family's history with such dignity."

"You are most welcome, ladies. I will let you know what the board decides."

Walking away from Iona's suitcase was cathartic. Her contents did not display the woman we knew she had become. Rather it indicated what her mother wanted her to become. Perhaps the suitcase was better left with the collection, for it didn't represent Iona as we knew her anyway.

Cat was another story. Her suitcase was not among the collection and her name was not listed among the patients residing at the asylum. Although Marlin was persistent, the health department was adamant that there was no such person at Willard.

We presumed from the letters we read that Cat was a nickname, but were never able to deduce a full name for the woman who would have been my great aunt. Delving into the bundles of correspondence became our priority in the succeeding days.

It was evident from the letters that Cat only had the education of a primary student. Conversely, Iona and Jennifer were both extremely well read and written. Iona detailed Daniel's growth and features as best she could to her friend. She detailed his first steps, his first words, and his likes and dislikes. She even included an imprint of his foot that she dipped in dye and stamped directly on the paper. Daniel was not a fussy baby and grew to be a strong, happy boy. His hair was fiery red, like Cat's, and he had her eyes as well. Iona included pencil drawings of Daniel whenever she sent a letter, and Cat always thanked her for doing so.

Cat's letters were short and concise and included drawings of her own that she labeled the back building. She did not live so much as exist in a world of torment. She often talked of her fears and drew pictures depicting them. One such letter had an image of the ghost that she claimed roamed the halls where she resided. Another had a drawing of a four-sided cage with the word "bad" written above it. Another image depicted a person being shackled to their bed, this time she wrote the word "Cat." It was in that particular letter that she also wrote the word "die." It was her wish to be put out of her misery. As time went on, her letters were even more pathetic. She described a fear of the back building, where patients were taken in shackles, never to return.

The final letter in the pile from Cat was a sympathy letter. In it, the administrator from the Willard Asylum indicated that Cat had passed away peacefully in her sleep. We highly doubted that but would never know now.

"Do you suppose she is buried there?" Marlin asked.

"I bet she is. I have read a great deal about the caretaker there. He was a man named Lawrence Marek. He was both the gravedigger and groundskeeper for over thirty years."

"Do you want to take a drive there? It's only about an hour away."

"Yes I would like that very much," Marlin said.

"Well then, we'll leave in the morning. We can grab some flowers on the way and pay our respects," I suggested.

When we arrived at the cemetery, we were immediately taken aback. The sign that greeted us indicated that over five thousand, seven hundred and seventy-six souls from Willard were laid to rest here. Patients with no family to claim them were often laid to rest on the grounds, as were patients whose families lacked the funds to transport their bodies home. Additionally, patients whose families were too ashamed to claim them were allowed them to be laid to rest where they resided.

The land was less like a cemetery and more like a large farmer's field. There were few memorial plaques but we were able to find small, round, unmarked graves that lay in the ground and were recognized only from their number.

"It's hard to believe we are standing on the ground where over five thousand people lay at rest. This is horrible. We need to do something about this," Marlin said, as tears streamed down her face.

"How are we supposed to find Cat without a marker of any kind, not even a headstone?" Camille chimed in.

"It's so sad. There is no other word. Regardless of whether or not the people who died here were mentally ill, they deserve proper memorials. The fact that they are disregarded is just wrong on every level," I said.

A woman approached us from the far corner of the field. She told us she was a volunteer for the Willard Cemetery Memorial Project, a group with good intentions to clean up the cemetery and restore it, complete with place markers and a listing of patients' names. She explained the appeals process she was going through with the Mental Health Department so that the deceased patients' names could be released. She walked us to a large boulder that was placed where Lawrence Merak's shack used to be. She told us the story of the gravedigger and the lengths they went to petition for a marker for him.

"Well, I suppose that's progress then if they allowed you to mark his home with this boulder."

"We aren't legally allowed to put his name on it, and if we do, I can be thrown in jail. So we have still have a long way to go."

"Well, we are happy to help," Marlin said, determined to stay a few weeks longer and help tidy the grounds. She even promised to raise funds for some new trees and pretty bushes.

CHAPTER TWENTY-EIGHT

JENNA

Jenna went from being a sweet and ordinary little girl who loved to play dress up and dolls, to a tormented child. The ghosts that haunted her, the eyeballs that surrounded her wherever she went and told her what to do ruled her life now. The eyeballs appeared out of nowhere, they were hidden in the walls or the upholstery of the couch she sat on. They stared at her when she lay in bed at night and woke her up first thing in the morning. The voices were everywhere too. The high-pitched little girl voice that loved desserts and movies, and the older male voice that scolded her for eating, never left her. She spoke to them too. They had a language that only they understood. She was riddled with anxiety and lived in chronic fear most likely as a result of the apparitions.

"She will require life-long maintenance in order to symptomatically manage and prevent the psychosis from reoccurring. I do believe the ECT therapy helped her case. Just last month her mood swings were more frequent and dire. When she became manic, she had wild hallucinations that people were trying to poison her and do her harm everywhere she went. That has ceased. She is still fearful and confused at times, but we are still working on her medication. There are other anti-psychotics we can try if we need to. We can couple medications too, try different combinations and find what works for her. It's not uncommon to transition from one med to the next every few years. Some of the medications can raise blood sugar and pressure levels, so we will watch that too."

"Will she ever lead a normal life, Dr. Saul?" Camille asked.

"I can't say for certain. On the plus side, we have caught and assessed this early. While other pediatric psychologists are reluctant to diagnose bipolar schizophrenia in adolescence because of the stigma, I think it gave us an advantage. We know what we are up against now and how to treat it. If we are vigilant with Jenna's care and keep her symptoms managed, she may be able to live normally, yes. Of course, we have to remain alert at all times."

"What about her education? Do they have schools for children like Jenna?"

"Part of Jenna's residential treatment program will include schooling. She will be bussed, with an aide, to a therapeutic day school. The staff is equipped to deal with mental illness of all kinds. You don't know how lucky you are, having a school and residential facility so close is rare."

"I wouldn't say we were lucky, but I know what you mean."

"She's not alone. Ten percent of the teens in the United States are dealing with some form of mental illness right now. If we can work to reduce the stigma that hovers above the term, we can save our children."

"Are they ready for her?" I asked, knowing Jenna would be getting antsy about starting her new journey.

"Yes they are. They have a bed ready and waiting, and a place set for her at the dinner table. You are welcome to stay for the meal and I encourage you to do so."

Jenna said goodbye to her favorite nurses' aide and came toward my daughter and me. She held Camille's hand, a good sign, and we got in the car together. My granddaughter was afraid of her own shadow now. She was a mere fraction of her former self. She was afraid to eat and battled her demons most often at mealtime. However, when we arrived at the facility we felt immediately at ease. The aide that came to meet us was gentle and kind. She connected with Jenna right away and helped her get situated in her room. She toured her around the home and asked her if there were any particular books she wished to read. They made weekly trips to the library and could get them next time for her.

When the dinner bell rang, several other children, ranging in age from eleven to sixteen, approached the dining room. Jenna was placed next to a boy with long shaggy hair and a lip ring. He was the oldest child in the home, but introduced himself to Jenna right away to make her feel welcome. It wasn't my business what his disorder was but I knew that among the kids residing here, there was sure to be those with severe anxiety, depression, bipolar, ADHD, PTSD, multiple personality disorder and schizophrenia. There would be those that wished to harm themselves or Jenna. Placing trust in such a situation took every ounce of strength I had.

Jenna was instructed along with the other kids to clasp her hands in the prayer position before the meal. Together the kids recited grace and anyone with difficulty calming down was instructed to close their eyes and take deep breaths while counting to one hundred.

Jenna was served a simple meal of chicken and biscuits, with vegetables on the side. She nibbled at the chicken, but dipped her biscuit into the gravy and ate more than half of it. She glanced around the table to assess the situation. I noticed that she kept swatting at her knee, the eyeballs were surely appearing in her skin telling her what to do. But she was controlling them, she was taking charge and holding her own.

Leaving Jenna was more challenging for my daughter and me, than it was for her. She did hug us goodbye and then a peculiar thing happened, she smiled. It was fleeting but it was there and my daughter and I both felt it. Her aide approached her and together they chose a TV show to watch before bedtime. The facility followed a strict schedule and believed routine was the key to the children's success.

"She's safe," I said when my daughter and I piled into the car.

Instead of going home, we went to a bar. I knocked back a shot of cherry-flavored vodka and Camille had a rum and coke.

To say relief washed over me and that my breath found a rhythm again when Jenna smiled would be like saying the sky was blue. I didn't realize how much I was holding in. I didn't recognize the constriction in my chest until it was gone and I could fill my lungs once again. The vodka stung my throat and warmed my chest. I ordered another.

We didn't ask for this life. But we are becoming versed in how to cope with what we have been given. Through the trials and tribulations, we have learned to embrace the joyous moments when they present themselves. We appreciate the smallest gestures, the kindness of strangers, the expertise of professionals, and the support of loved ones.

I used to say flippant things all the time like, "that's insane," "you're crazy," or don't be a "psychopath." However, now I choose my words more carefully so that I don't undermine the disease of mental illness that crippled my grandmother and now my granddaughter. If we can replace the stigmas with compassion, patience, and general kindness then maybe afflicted individuals like Jenna and Noah, Iona and Cat, may feel more safe and at ease in the world.

BOOK STUDY QUESTIONS

1. The book is divided into sections, the past is Part 1 and the present is Part 2. If the story were written from only one time period, which would you choose and why?

2. The suitcases that were discovered left behind at Willard in 1995 were the impetus for this story. Had you heard about them?Discuss how the discovery may have impacted the mental health community today.

3. If you were sent away in the year 1915, what would be found in your suitcase? What would be different if you packed it today?

4. Iona represents a strong young female who is sent away to an asylum for disobedience, among other things. When she is targeted by Fatty Patty and becomes tormented daily, she reacts violently. Is this a sign of strength, or weakness? How else might she have reacted?

5. Fatty Patty firmly believed that the devil was in Iona, and was abusive in her quest to "cleanse" her. Was Patty a bad" person, or did she truly believe that starving and depriving patients of their basic human needs would help them to heal?

6. Do you think Iona would have been able to lead a good life that included having a family of her own without James and Jennifer?How did they impact her ability to do this?

7. Discuss the differences between Cat and Iona. Do you feel empathetic towards either one of them given their circumstances?

8. There is a stigma that surrounds mental illness, it was evident both in 1915 and still remains today. As a result of the stigma, the cemetery at the Willard Insane Asylum is unkempt and does not even have markers for the deceased, instead it has numbers or, in some cases, blank stones. What does this say about our culture? Discuss the government's role (including the HIPAA laws) in this dilemma and whether or not it hurts or helps the plight of removing the stigma from the disease.

9. Discuss what it means to be "normal". Further discuss how percep-tions of being "normal" impact our society as a whole.

10. How would you like to see Jenna's story unfold?

SUBSCRIBER LINK

If you like this book and you wish to join my mailing list for new releases, please visit my website www.juliedewey.com.

Author's photo by Marnie Carter

ABOUT THE AUTHOR

Julie Dewey is a novelist residing in Central New York with her family. Julie selects book topics that are little known nuggets of U.S. history and sheds light on them so that the reader not only gets an intriguing storyline but learns a little something too.

In addition to reading, researching, and writing, Julie has many hobbies that include jewelry design, decorating, walking her favorite four legged friends, Wells and Hershey, and spending time with her triplet nephews.

Her works include *Forgetting Tabitha, Train Rider,*
The Back Building, One Thousand Porches,
The Other Side of the Fence, and *Cat (the Livin' Large Series).*

To follow Julie visit www.juliedewey.com and sign up to get regular updates and reading guides.